"I'm really sorry I made a scene in front of all your modeling friends. But it was worth the embarrassment. I think I've been discovered!"

"What?"

"You know, like Lana Turner, that movie star who was drinking a soda at the right drug store. That guy, he gave me his card."

"*Comment*? What are you talking about?" Nicole pushed the elevator button and turned to stare at her sister in surprise.

"The photographer," Mollie sighed, still ecstatic over her unexpected good fortune. "He says I may be just right for a new sitcom! I'm going to be on television, Nicole!"

"*Mon dieu!*" Nicole said, ignoring the open elevator door as she gazed at Mollie in horror. What had she started now?

FAWCETT GIRLS ONLY BOOKS

SISTERS

SISTERS

STAR QUALITY

Jennifer Cole

FAWCETT GIRLS ONLY • NEW YORK

RLI:
VL: Grades 6 + up
IL: Grades 7 + up

A Fawcett Girls Only Book
Published by Ballantine Books
Copyright © 1986 by Cloverdale Press, Inc.

Library of Congress Catalog Card Number: 86-91297

ISBN 0-449-13207-2

Manufactured in the United States of America

First Edition: January 1987

Chapter 1

"Cindy! Look at this!" Mollie Lewis shouted to her older sister as she danced an impromptu jig around the kitchen table.

Cindy pulled off the earphones that her father swore were permanently attached to her head, and stared at Mollie in astonishment. "You're dropping the mail all over the floor," she said. "What is it? Did you win a million dollars in one of those magazine sweepstakes?"

Fourteen-year-old Mollie—diverted by the thought of instant wealth—paused for a moment, then resumed her victory dance. "No, this is even better. Come and see."

Cindy put down her half-eaten sandwich and walked across the spacious kitchen to examine the source of Mollie's excitement.

"That's just a circular from Parkstone," she said, shaking her head in disappointment. Mollie could certainly make a fuss about the dumbest things. What was so interesting about a department store ad? "I thought you had something really spectacular; I'm not interested in the latest dress sale."

Mollie grinned at her tall, athletically trim sister, who lived in jeans and ragged cutoffs. "Of course not, considering that you once stood up the cutest boy at Vista High just because you were afraid to turn up at a dance in a formal gown—"

"I didn't stand him up, I had a good reason," Cindy protested, "and besides—"

"Never mind." Mollie waved the colorful brochure in front of her. "Look at this!"

"I don't see what you're so excited about," Cindy said with a frown. But then her mouth dropped open in surprise and she let out a loud whoop. "It's Nicole!"

"Doesn't she look absolutely beautiful?" Mollie sighed, the admiration in her voice tinged with just a trace of envy. They both stared at the photo of their oldest sister. Nicole looked gorgeous in a mauve-and-pink sweater and matching skirt. Despite her seventeen years, she also looked incredibly mature as she gazed out at them from the front of the circular.

"I don't even remember hearing about this job," Mollie said.

"I thought she was only going to model in the summer, anyway."

"No, she talked Mom and Dad into allowing her to do a few extra assignments," Cindy explained.

"You know Nicole; she can always twist them around her little finger."

The back door slammed as a voice rang out, "I heard that!"

Both girls looked up to see Nicole entering the kitchen, her arms full of books. She paused in the doorway, a little startled by her sisters' inquisitive gaze, not realizing that they were comparing her to her picture. Even after a long day at school, Nicole still looked cool and serene. Her brown hair fell in a soft wave across her cheek and her blue eyes sparkled with the slightest hint of makeup.

It wasn't fair, Mollie thought glumly. Nicole had always been pretty, but after the modeling course she had taken a few months back, she had become almost too perfect to live with—especially for Mollie, who was three years younger, and considered herself too short and verging on the perilous edge of overweight.

"What's the matter?" Nicole demanded now. "Why are you frowning at me, Mollie?"

"Why do you have to be so perfect?" Mollie wailed. "And why am I so fat?"

Nicole laughed and looked at her petite younger sister affectionately. "You're not fat, you dummy! You have a lovely figure. You know perfectly well the boys like you just as you are!"

"You think so?" Mollie's expression brightened.

"Yes, of course I think so. What's that, a new diet plan?" Nicole teased when she noticed the brochure Mollie was holding. She dropped her books on the counter and started toward the refrigerator for some fruit juice.

"You haven't seen it? Look!" Mollie waved the brochure in front of her sister's face and Nicole paused to look.

"Mon dieu!" Nicole grabbed the sheet, shivering with excitement as she scanned the glossy advertisement. Although she had had one earlier modeling assignment, the ad had not yet made it into print, and this was the first time she had seen the results of one of her sessions. She felt almost as awed as her sisters.

Cindy and Mollie, familiar with Nicole's French expressions, watched as she stared at her own photograph in wonder, finally sighing, "I don't look bad, do I?"

Mollie groaned. "You look incredibly beautiful, you rat fink! I should look so good." She reached for the brochure. "Give it back, I'm taking it to school tomorrow to show my friends."

Nicole released the ad reluctantly, and Mollie marched out of the room, completely forgetting the slice of cheesecake she had taken from the fridge.

"Mollie, what about your snack?" Nicole called after her.

"Forget it—I'm going on a diet."

"Again? When did this one start?" Cindy snorted.

"As soon as I saw my sister the model," Mollie answered from the hall.

"You really do look good in that ad, Nicole," Cindy told her sister. "How did you talk Mom and Dad into letting you model before school's out?"

Nicole made a face. "I promised them I would only do an occasional shoot, and *not* let it interfere with my schoolwork this time. I need to build up my college fund again. You can't model without a portfolio to send around, and I just about wiped out my savings account having my pictures taken; photographers don't work for peanuts."

"Or cheesecake," Cindy agreed, deciding not to let the abandoned slice go to waste. She reached for the plate. "Want a bite?"

Nicole looked at the rich dessert wistfully. Their mother, who operated a very successful catering business, Movable Feast, made a cheesecake that could win prizes—and often did. "I'd better not."

"*You're* on a diet?" Cindy looked up in surprise. Her slim, graceful sister didn't need to count calories.

"No, I'm just being careful," Nicole explained. She watched her sister dig into the dessert and sighed.

"In Mollie's hands, that ad will be all over school tomorrow," Cindy pointed out. "If you're ever rich and famous, you won't need a public relations manager, Nicole. You've got one in the family already."

Upstairs in her bedroom, Mollie pushed aside a pile of abandoned clothing and threw herself onto her unmade bed. She spread the advertisement out in front of her and gazed once more at her perfect sister, caught by the camera's magic in an eternally graceful pose.

"It's not fair," she repeated. "If I'd been the

oldest—the slim, tall one—it would be me in that picture right now." She rested her chin in her palms and pondered the unfairness of fate.

A clump-clump on the carpeted stairs announced the arrival of Winston, the Lewises' Newfoundland, but Mollie hardly noticed. Not until his friendly wet muzzle pushed against her neck did Mollie put one hand out to ruffle the black fur.

"Hi, Winnie," she greeted the dog. "I forgot to bring you a snack. Sorry. Guess you'll have to diet along with me."

Puzzled, the big dog settled down onto the carpet beside the bed. Mollie reached out to stroke him. "You can save me from the cold, Winnie, but you can't make me beautiful like Nicole."

Winston had been the recipient of extraspecial petting ever since his role in averting Mollie's near-disaster during the Lewis family's ski trip in Lake Tahoe. Now he lifted his ears at the mention of his name, but with no food in sight, he settled back into a comfortable position on the soft carpet.

Mollie reached absently for a half-eaten candy bar, then remembered, and pushed it firmly away. "Here, Winnie, you can have this. Nicole would say it's bad for your teeth, but I won't tell."

The big dog gobbled down the tidbit in one gulp, licked Mollie's hand in appreciation, then flopped back down to the floor.

Mollie, unable to eat away her depression, decided to do the next best thing and reach for the telephone to call her best friend.

"Sarah? It's Mollie," she said when the connection was made. "Has your mail come yet? Go and get the circular from Parkstone Department Store."

"What for?"

"Just do it." Mollie waited, chewing on one nail as she studied the picture in front of her.

"Okay, I got it, now what? Did you find the perfect dress?"

"Look at the front page," Mollie advised.

"Wow! That's Nicole!"

"You got it," Mollie responded glumly. "Exciting, isn't it?"

"I think it's terrific. But you don't sound too pleased."

"I am, really," Mollie assured her. "It's just that— Sarah, when I was little and thought everybody was picking on me, I used to pretend I was Cinderella, with two awful stepsisters. I pretended that one day they'd realize how unfair they'd been, the prince would fall in love with me, and everything in my life would be perfect from then on. But the stepsisters are supposed to be *ugly*! I can't be Cinderella with a gorgeous model for a sister. It makes me feel like an ugly duckling."

"But, Mollie," her friend comforted, "ugly ducklings turn into swans. You know that."

"Not this one," Mollie grumbled. "With my luck, I'll probably get plucked for Sunday dinner."

Sarah laughed and Mollie glared at the receiver in her hand. "It's not funny!"

"Yes, it is. You're not the least bit ugly, and you know it. You told me after you found out about Nicole's modeling lessons that you were going to take a modeling class, too. So why don't you do it now?"

"I don't have any money left," Mollie confessed. "Mom made me pay her back for part of that stuff I bought in Tahoe; she said it was my own fault I left all my winter clothes at home just because I didn't want to go. Anyhow, I know what Mom and Dad would say—'You're too young.' "

"So, who needs lessons? You're not exactly inexperienced. Look how good you were in the fall play. If you could walk across the stage in front of an audience playing the lead in *Grease*, surely you can pose in front of one little camera."

Mollie's spirits began to lift. "You really think so?"

"I'm positive. I bet you'd knock their socks off."

"Sarah, you're a great friend, you know that?" Mollie heard her friend giggle.

"Instant ego build-up by Dr. Sarah. You'll get my bill tomorrow."

"You creep," Mollie said. Then, feeling more like her usual exuberant self, she and Sarah began to discuss strategies for turning her into the second Lewis sister to stun the fashion world.

She was still on the phone when Nicole knocked on her door a little while later. "Dinner's almost ready. Where's that ad? I want to show Mom and Dad."

Mollie handed over the brochure and hung up the receiver. "Nicole," she called after her sister, but the older girl had already started down the stairway. "Darn."

Mollie ran to pull a brush through her tangled

blond curls, then headed for the stairs. The phone rang just as she reached the living room and she picked up the receiver automatically. Mollie could see Cindy in the dining room setting the table. She sniffed at an especially savory aroma drifting in from the kitchen, then said, "Hello? Lewis residence. Uh, hold on." She put her hand over the receiver and yelled toward the kitchen, "Hey, Nicole, it's for you. I think it's the guy from the modeling agency."

Nicole hurried out into the hall.

"Mollie, don't be so gauche!" She took the phone away from her sister, raising her eyebrows as she spoke in a carefully modulated tone. "Hello, Alain. *Qu'est-ce que comment!* Really? Are you sure? *Ne quittez pas.*"

She lowered the receiver to glare at Mollie. "If you don't mind, this is a private conversation!"

"I can take a hint," Mollie pouted, limping toward the dining room.

"Is your ankle still bothering you, Mollie?" Mrs. Lewis asked, as she carried a large serving dish in from the kitchen.

"She's just doing that because she feels sorry for herself. That smells scrumptious." Cindy sniffed appreciatively at the steam still rising from the hot dish as her mother set it carefully onto a silver trivet. "I'm starved."

"Even after that huge sandwich you wolfed down after school?" Mollie, jealous of her tomboyish sister who could eat anything without gaining an ounce, wrinkled her brow.

"That was hours ago," Cindy countered.

"We're almost ready," their mother said quickly, to avoid a squabble. "Call your father. Where's Nicole?"

"On the phone." Mollie limped toward the hallway. "I'll get Dad." She tossed her blond curls. "Even if it *does* make my ankle worse to do all the errands around here!"

"Oh, Mollie." Laura Lewis shook her head.

"Just ignore her, Mom," Cindy said. "Maybe she'll go away."

When they all gathered around the dining table, and both parents had exclaimed over the advertisement, Mrs. Lewis began to dish out the steaming hot beef stroganoff.

"None for me, Mom." Nicole pulled her plate back hastily. "Just salad and a little of the fruit compote."

"Aren't you feeling well, Nicole?" Richard Lewis peered at his oldest daughter over his glass.

"I'm fine, Dad. But Alain called, and they have another assignment for me."

Her father frowned, and Mrs. Lewis put down the ladle. "Nicole, you know we agreed that you wouldn't get carried away with your modeling; we don't want you to forget that school is still your top priority. Senior year is most important. Even if you *have* been accepted at Smith and Vassar, you don't want your grades to drop now."

"Oh, Mom, I won't, *vraiment*! But Alain says this is a great assignment, and they really want me— they said I was perfect!"

Mollie, watching her mother waver, poked a fork at her own salad. Was this fair? Nicole was becoming sought after already; what chance did that leave the youngest Lewis?

"They're going to schedule the shoot for Saturday morning. I won't even miss any school."

Laura Lewis glanced at her husband and they came to a silent agreement. "All right. But remember what I said about priorities."

"I will, Mom." Nicole glowed with excitement, and Mollie saw her father look fondly at his oldest daughter.

"None for me either, Mom," Mollie said as her mother continued serving.

"For goodness' sake," Mrs. Lewis protested, "isn't anyone eating tonight? What about all this stroganoff?"

"I'm not on any silly diet," Cindy reminded her, holding out her plate. "Pile it on."

They all laughed, but Nicole regarded her youngest sister warily. "What kind of a diet is it this time, Mollie? Bananas for three straight days?"

"That was last month." Mollie's tone was lofty. "I don't want David to think I'm getting too fat."

Nicole raised her brows. "David seems to like you just the way you are." She delicately smoothed her napkin across her lap. "He's pretty cute himself."

Mollie brightened momentarily, thinking of the blond sophomore. They were just good friends, but she did like him a lot. "He is cute, isn't he?" She sighed, then remembered her real motivation. "If I lose five pounds this week, would you talk to your agent about a modeling job for me, Nicole?"

"*Mon dieu,*" Nicole murmured. "I should have guessed."

"Mollie." Laura Lewis's expression was alarmed. "It's difficult enough for Nicole to manage schoolwork and a part-time job. I really don't think you're ready for that kind of juggling act just yet."

"You always say I'm too young!" Mollie's voice rose, and tears filled her eyes. "You think just because I'm the youngest, I can't do anything!"

Mrs. Lewis chose her words carefully. "It's not that we don't have faith in you, sweetheart. But you do tend to overestimate your own abilities sometimes. I don't think you're ready for this."

"Yes, I am," Mollie insisted stubbornly. "I know I could be just as good at modeling as Nicole." She eyed her slim sister, and sighed. "Well, almost. Nicole, won't you please—"

"Absolutely not!"

Chapter 2

When her alarm buzzed Friday morning, Nicole groped for the off button, yawned, and pushed herself up from her Laura Ashley sheets. Grabbing her robe, she headed for the bathroom, intent on getting into the shower before Cindy got there first. She grabbed a thick towel from the linen closet, then paused in disbelief.

Large white letters, apparently fashioned from their dad's shaving cream, marched across the bathroom mirror: NICOLE, PLEASE HELP ME!

Nicole groaned. It was too early in the morning to face her sister's demands. "How did she get up early enough to do this?" Nicole wondered aloud. Mollie's aversion to getting up early was well known in the Lewis family.

Cindy grinned as she reached around Nicole to pull out her toothbrush. "She did it last night. I saw her on my way to bed."

"Mon dieu." Nicole shook her head and opened the shower door.

But Mollie had only just begun.

A little while later, Nicole, fully dressed, her bed made and her room in perfect order, gathered her school books and her purse and headed downstairs. She pushed through the swinging door into the kitchen, then stopped short. A full place setting, complete with half a grapefruit and a thermos of coffee, was laid out at her seat. In front of her plate was a large, hand-lettered sign: FOR MY FAVORITE SISTER.

"Oh, dear," Nicole sighed, examining the breakfast with misgivings. "Don't tell me she did this last night, too."

Cindy, eating a large bowl of cereal at the other end of the table, laughed. "How did you guess?"

Nicole looked at the dried-up grapefruit with distaste and murmured, "It wasn't hard." She opened the thermos and poured out the coffee. It still felt moderately warm, but the liquid looked thick enough to pave the street outside. Nicole shuddered as Mollie, looking unusually lively for such an early hour, bounded into the kitchen.

"Hi, guys," she said, turning a hopeful eye toward Nicole. "How's the coffee?"

"Fine." Nicole, with Mollie's eyes upon her, forced herself to take a sip of the murky black liquid and barely repressed a shudder. "But I've got to rush. I'm late."

"It's only seven-thirty," Mollie protested, disappointed at seeing her efforts go unappreciated.

"I've, uh . . . got a yearbook meeting before

school. Thanks for the breakfast, Mollie. See you later."

Nicole looked into the refrigerator to retrieve a lunch she had packed the night before, grabbed her books, and hurried out the door.

Behind her, Cindy smiled at the crestfallen Mollie. "Nice try, shrimp."

Mollie managed a weak grin and considered eating the grapefruit herself. If this was typical model's fare, perhaps she had better get used to it. She took one bite of the shriveled fruit and grimaced at the sharp taste. On the other hand, she didn't have to start just yet, she told herself, and cinnamon toast sounded awfully good. She headed for the pantry, in search of cinnamon, sugar, and bread.

When Nicole arrived at Vista High, she found her friend Bitsy waiting by her locker, holding the advertising circular in her hand.

"Nicole, you look beautiful. I couldn't believe it was really you!"

"Thanks, I think."

"You know what I mean," Bitsy protested, juggling her books and the ad as Nicole opened her locker and exchanged her history textbook for her French one. "Aren't you excited?"

"It gave me a funny feeling when I saw it," Nicole admitted. "It seems a little unreal, even to me. You really think I look good?"

"Listen to her!" Bitsy exclaimed to no one in particular, looking from the advertisement to her own outfit, unable to avoid making a comparison.

Even this early in the day, she had somehow managed to rumple her blouse, and a stain of unknown origin blotted the knee of her almost new slacks. She ran a hand through her short blond hair and sighed. "You make me feel like an also-ran."

Nicole laughed. "Cut it out, Bitsy. You look really nice in that shade of blue."

"Honest?" Her friend brightened, but she couldn't be diverted. "You're probably going to be the next Christie Brinkley. I wish I could have my picture on the front of a magazine!"

"You wouldn't if you had a little sister," Nicole warned. "Now Mollie wants to be a model, too. She's driving me nuts."

"Oh, Nicole, you know Mollie. She has a different ambition every other day. She'll get over it."

"I hope so, or I'm going to have to give up eating breakfast entirely," Nicole grumbled, then grinned at her friend's puzzled expression. "Come on, I'll tell you about my morning so far."

Although Nicole received many more compliments on her first released modeling venture throughout the morning, it didn't thrill her to catch a glimpse of Mollie at the end of the hall, surrounded by what appeared to be at least half the freshman class. Mollie was proudly displaying the eye-catching advertising circular.

"You're certainly going to be famous at Vista High," Bitsy said with a laugh, "if nowhere else."

Nicole ducked her head and hurried into the

cafeteria, afraid that her fame was getting out of hand.

"Did you bring lunch?" Bitsy spotted the brown bag and couldn't conceal her interest. All of the Lewis sisters' friends knew about Laura Lewis's fantastic cooking. "What have you got?"

"Mother had some goodies left over from an anniversary dinner yesterday, so I grabbed some miniature quiches and stuffed mushrooms."

Bitsy groaned, and Nicole grinned at her friend. "You can have some."

But when she opened the bag, on top of the neat, foil-wrapped packages, Nicole discovered a large sheet of white paper with a handwritten note printed out in neat, colorful lettering.

"Nicole—please, please, please reconsider!" Bitsy read over her shoulder. "My goodness, is that from Mollie?"

Nicole nodded. "I feel like Scrooge being hounded by all the Christmas ghosts. I never know when another spirit is going to appear."

Bitsy, who had just popped a stuffed mushroom into her mouth, almost choked. "Don't make me laugh with my mouth full. What are you going to do about Mollie?"

"Je ne sais pas!" Nicole groaned. "I just don't know."

"Do you think Mollie could model successfully? I'd like to be a model, too, but I thought models had to be tall," Bitsy pointed out.

"She won't listen to me. You know Mollie when she gets an idea into her stubborn head."

"Maybe you *should* talk to Alain about Mollie,

then," Bitsy said shrewdly. "She'll *have* to listen
to him."

"C'est le vrai." Nicole nodded slowly. "You may
be right."

After school that day, Nicole approached the
sprawling, Spanish-style Lewis home with unac-
customed reluctance. She considered dropping
off her books and slipping away again, but decided against it. She wouldn't be driven away
from home by her own sister. But when she cautiously pushed open the back door, a petite figure
jumped up from a kitchen stool to confront her.

"Nicole!"

"Who else?" Nicole gazed warily at her youngest sister, waiting to see what new variation of
her familiar plea Mollie had devised.

"Mrs. Washington said that I could do my theme
for English class on what it's like to be a model.
Just think—you'll be helping me get a good grade."

"Fat lot you care about grades! That's plain
blackmail, Mollie!" Nicole sounded indignant.

Mollie, afraid she might have gone too far, bit
her lip as she watched her sister drop her books
onto the counter.

"You had no right to tell your teacher that you
were going to model when I haven't even agreed
to speak to Alain about you!"

"I didn't—I mean, I didn't really say that the
essay would be about *me*," Mollie confessed. "I
showed her your ad and she was very impressed.
I'm sorry, Nicole. I know I've been a pest, but I
really want to model."

Nicole, watching Mollie's hopeful smile fade, felt her irritation dissolve. It was hopeless, she told herself. She might as well relent with good grace before Mollie drove her completely mad.

"I'll speak to Alain," she began, holding out one hand to stop Mollie, who had begun to do a dance around the kitchen. "I only said I'll talk to him; that doesn't mean he will see you, and even if he does, he may not think you're right for modeling, Mollie."

"At least I'll have a chance," Mollie shouted, beside herself with excitement. "Thank you, Nicole. You're the best sister in the whole world!"

Mollie nearly tripped over Smokey, one of the two Lewis cats, then regained her balance and headed upstairs to call her friends with the wonderful news. She was moving at a fast clip when she passed Cindy on her way downstairs for a snack.

Cindy grinned at Nicole as she entered the kitchen.

"Gave in, huh?"

"Mollie could wear down a mountain! She's about as close to an irresistible force as I want to encounter."

"Look on the bright side," Cindy said, opening the refrigerator door. "You won't have to drink any more of her coffee."

On Friday afternoon, Nicole stood in the doorway of Mollie's room and tapped her foot impatiently.

"Mollie, we've got to go!"

Mollie, almost hidden behind the pile of clothing that covered her bed, was pulling on her fifth pair of shoes. "How does this look, Nicole?"

"You look fine. You looked fine in the first outfit, the second, and the third. But if you don't hurry up, Alain will have left the office by the time we get there. He's only doing this as a favor to me. And if Mother finds out I got you out of school an hour early, she'll kill me. So let's go."

Mollie reappeared from behind the pile of abandoned garments, her face heavily made up. Nicole shook her head. But there was no more time to fix up her exasperating little sister properly.

"I'm leaving. If you're going with me, be at the corner in five minutes."

Mollie gave one last anguished look at herself in the bedroom mirror and thought, Maybe I should have worn the peach and green outfit after all. Then she ran down the steps and tore after her sister.

Once they had boarded the bus, Mollie cast an anxious glance at Nicole.

"I really appreciate this, you know. Honestly."

"You'd better," Nicole answered irritably, watching the traffic as they headed toward the center of town. "If Alain weren't such a nice guy, he wouldn't have bothered with either of us."

Mollie swallowed hard and tried to remember how simple becoming a sought-after model had seemed from the safety of her bedroom. Yesterday the idea had appeared perfectly sane, but today she was experiencing a serious case of butterflies. Now that she was really on her way to face inspection by a real modeling agent, Mollie felt much less certain of her star appeal.

She looked at Nicole, so poised and confident, looking much older than her seventeen years.

"You don't think I'm ugly, do you, Nicole?"

"Of course not, dummy."

Nicole squeezed Mollie's hand. Just when she was ready to strangle her sister for being such a demanding brat, Mollie would look at her with that lost, wistful expression. It was as if she were a chubby toddler again, following her older sister everywhere, wailing, "Wait for me, N'cole."

And Nicole would melt, just as she always had. Darn little sisters, anyhow, Nicole thought.

"I can't guarantee what Alain will say, Mollie," she said for the tenth time. "He may not take you on."

"I know, I know," Mollie said, trying to cross all of her fingers at once. She braced herself against the sway of the bus and counted the intersections.

By the time they entered the stark, futuristic black-and-white waiting area of the modeling agency, Mollie's courage had shrunk to the size of a pea. She hung back while Nicole spoke to the receptionist, sinking meekly into a chair that resembled a giant mushroom.

"Alain will be with you in a minute," Nicole told her.

"No hurry," Mollie whispered.

Nicole grinned at Mollie's change in attitude, shaking her head at the quaver in her sister's voice.

"He's not going to eat you, Mollie. Take a deep breath and relax."

"If I do, I'll disappear into this thing and never be seen again." Mollie struggled to sit upright on the soft cushions.

Nicole giggled. Mollie did look a bit like a brightly colored elf perched on a black toadstool.

Just then the inner door opened, and a tall man in an expertly tailored suit appeared in the doorway, his dark hair sprinkled with gray.

"Mollie Lewis?"

"Here," Mollie murmured, instinctively looking to Nicole for support. But her sister shook her head.

"Go on in, Mollie. I'll wait here."

Mollie, afraid that Alain would see the tremor in her knees, held herself straight with great effort. It seemed like a mile from her chair to his office, but then she was shaking his hand and being ushered into the inner sanctum.

Alain waved her into a more conventional chair while he took his seat behind a huge desk of pale wood. Mollie glanced at the wall behind him which was covered with pictures—blondes, brunettes, redheads of all ages—all looking infinitely more attractive and interesting than Mollie Lewis had ever looked. She swallowed hard.

"So you would like to be a model, *n'est-ce pas?*"

No wonder Nicole gets along so well with this guy, Mollie thought irreverently. He likes French expressions, too. Though from his slight accent, she thought his way of speaking might be a bit more natural than Nicole's affectations. She nodded, afraid to trust her voice.

Alain seemed to sense her nervousness and flashed her a reassuring smile. If she hadn't been frozen with utter terror, Mollie would have found him awfully good-looking in an attractive older-man way.

"How tall are you, Mollie?"

Mollie pulled herself out of her daydream abruptly. "Five feet exactly," she said.

"Weight?"

Mollie hesitated, wondering if she could shave off a few pounds. The man behind the desk seemed to read her thought.

"We have a doctor's scale in the dressing room if you're not sure."

Mollie blushed, sure that her attempt at subterfuge was painfully obvious.

"Never mind that just now. Stand up, please, Mollie, and turn around slowly."

Mollie, her face still flushed, did as she was told, then looked back at Alain, holding her breath.

"You're a very attractive young lady, my dear," Alain began kindly. "But, unfortunately, not really the type that we need at the moment. The models most in demand are slightly taller than you."

Mollie bit her lip hard, trying to hold back a rush of tears. "I see," she managed to say. "Thank you for seeing me anyhow, sir."

"You're quite welcome." Alain stood up again and ushered her toward the door. "I'm sure you'll find success doing something else, Mollie."

Nicole stood up when Mollie reappeared and

gave her sister an inquiring glance. The younger girl shook her head slightly, still not trusting her voice. When they were safely in the elevator, with the doors closed behind them, Mollie wailed, "He said I'm not the right type, Nicole!"

"I warned you, Mollie," Nicole said, relieved but trying to sound sympathetic, too. "Not everyone is cut out for modeling. Don't be too disappointed."

"Easy for you to say," Mollie sniffed. "But this is not the only modeling agency in California, Nicole. Maybe someone else would be interested in me."

"Don't even think it, Mollie!" Nicole turned on her sister with such fervor that Mollie jumped. "Some of those ads in the papers for models are placed by people who aren't legitimate. Modeling is not what they're interested in at all!"

"What do you mean?" Mollie, genuinely puzzled, stared at her sister's alarmed expression.

"Never mind; just take my word for it!" The usually gentle Nicole sounded so vehement that Mollie didn't press her.

"Okay, okay," she said. Mollie was silent as she trudged after her sister toward the bus stop. On the ride home, she appeared deep in thought, but she surprised Nicole by jumping up from her seat before they had reached their stop.

"What are you doing?" Nicole asked.

"Getting off at the library."

Nicole watched her sister step off the bus, and turn toward the public library. Maybe she'll find something else to think about, Nicole thought to herself, a little surprised that Mollie was taking Alain's rejection so well.

As the bus pulled away, Nicole's thoughts shifted to her own modeling career, and the new assignment coming up. Mollie would be all right, she assured herself. She always snapped back quickly from one of her crazy schemes. But Nicole would have been less relieved if she had seen her sister inside the library, skimming through a thick volume entitled *The Entertainment Industry from A to Z.*

Chapter 3

A loud buzzing disrupted Nicole's dreamless sleep. She struggled to open her eyes, then groaned with annoyance, reached out one hand, and finally managed to turn off the alarm. Prying one eye open, she stared into the darkness. The digital clock on her bedside table read five A.M. Why had she set the alarm so early?

Memory flooded back, and Nicole sat straight up in bed, her heart suddenly pounding with excitement. She had a modeling job today! It would be her first outdoor shoot, and she had to meet the photographer in less than an hour to catch the early morning sunshine. Slipping hurriedly out of bed, she ran for the shower.

By the time Nicole got downstairs, tiptoeing on the carpeted steps in order not to wake anyone, there was no time for breakfast. *Just as well,* Nicole thought. Her stomach already quivered with nervousness. But she could certainly use a cup of coffee. Not enough time to turn on the coffee machine; she didn't even have time to boil water. She could not be late. Forgoing even a glass of orange juice, Nicole skipped out the door and groped her way in the darkness to the garage.

She backed the family station wagon out of the driveway and into the street. The beachfront park where they were scheduled to shoot was only a fifteen-minute drive from her house, and Nicole found the location without difficulty. She parked beside a couple of large vans and got out of the car.

The door to the first van was open and inside Nicole caught a glimpse of an enormous array of cameras and other equipment. A middle-aged photographer loaded film into a large camera, while another man—the art director—stood beside the van and swore under his breath at the low morning clouds. Several other people were busy setting up props and adjusting reflectors.

"I told you there'd be fog. Didn't I tell you?"

"It's not really fog, just a bit misty. It'll make a nice, dreamy look in the pictures," the photographer said cheerfully.

"But it won't look like spring!"

"Relax, Harry," the man inside the van said over his shoulder. "It's lifting already. The sunlight will be strong enough, I think. We'll take a couple of test shots as soon as I get set up."

"Hello," Nicole said, trying to look more confident than she felt. "I'm Nicole Lewis, one of the models."

The man outside nodded and waved toward the other van. "The clothes are in there; you girls will use that for a dressing room. Get a move on, Nicky. The light—such as it is—waits for nobody."

"Yes sir." Nicole approached the other van and knocked on the back door.

"Who is it?" a muffled voice asked.

"Nicole—one of the models."

"Just a sec."

Nicole waited patiently, shivering slightly as the breeze off the ocean touched her with its damp chill. Finally the voice called out, "Come on in."

Nicole opened the door and climbed awkwardly inside, weaving her way around boxes and racks of clothing. In the front of the crowded space, stood a slender blonde who looked several years older than Nicole.

"Hi, I'm Christine."

"Hello," Nicole answered, smiling hesitantly. "Which outfit am I supposed to wear?"

"Try this one; if Harry doesn't like the look of it, he'll let you know fast enough."

Nicole began to pull off her thick sweater, looking dubiously at the thin sundress that Christine had pointed out. "We're going to freeze to death out there."

"Just be thankful we're not modeling swim suits." Christine grinned.

Nicole nodded in fervent agreement and began to pull on the dress.

As soon as Nicole finished dressing, the makeup

artist applied cosmetics to her face, and then the hairstylist had his turn with her.

"Let's go, girls!"

As they pushed open the door, Christine and Nicole were assaulted by a rush of ice-cold air. They both shivered as they felt the bite of the wind. Nicole put her hands to her head, trying to keep the stylist's careful job in place.

"Over here in front of the palm trees," the art director ordered, and they hastened to obey, tottering across the sand in their high heels.

They achieved a decent pose in the designated spot, only to have the photographer look up from his large camera and shake his head. "That's boring, Harry."

"Where are the other props?"

"In the van."

"Let's try a beach ball."

One of the assistants hurried to bring out some props, and the photographer positioned them again. Nicole, hoping that her goose bumps wouldn't show, tried to smile naturally at the camera as she tossed the ball back and forth with Christine. But then the art director decided that the orange and white beach ball clashed with the peach-colored sundress, and the models had to stand and wait again while the men behind the cameras discussed the composition of the picture.

"Try the parasol," one of the assistants suggested.

Nicole knew that it was going to be a long day.

By the time they finished shooting, the sun was high in the sky. Although Nicole hadn't been able to wear her watch during the session, she was sure it was nearly noon. Her stomach felt uncomfortably empty, and the rest of her felt lightheaded and dizzy. Her back ached from posing for hours in high heels, and she was so cold from the chilly sea breeze that her hands and feet were totally numb.

They had collected several spectators as the day wore on, and Nicole spotted a couple of her friends from Vista High. She waved to them as she rushed off to the van to change clothes, and tried to smile. Probably Bitsy and the others thought she was having a great time. Nicole tried to look the part, but she was too tired.

When the photographer at last called it a day, Nicole and Christine looked at each other in relief.

"Thank heaven," Nicole murmured to the other girl. "I thought I'd turn into a block of ice."

"Just wait till you have to pose in snowsuits in July," Christine joked.

Nicole pulled off the beach hat that had perched on her head—and had taken at least fifteen minutes to be adjusted to just the right angle—and ran for the van.

Back in her own clothes, she hung up the two-piece beach outfit she had been modeling, and stepped outside the van.

"See you, Christine."

"Hope next time we're indoors," the other girl called after her.

Nicole nodded fervently. She was surprised to see Alain waiting for her, leaning casually against her car. He was holding two steaming paper cups, and a delectable aroma greeted Nicole as she hurried to greet him.

"For me?"

"Mais oui." Alain held out one of the cups of coffee and Nicole took it eagerly. She took a swallow, burned her tongue, then sipped more cautiously. It didn't have cream and sugar as she would have liked, but it was hot.

"You saved my life," she told the agent. *"Merci beaucoup!"*

"How did it go this morning?"

"All right, I guess." Nicole looked doubtfully toward the other van, where the photographer and his assistant were repacking the equipment. "I don't know how good I was."

Alain chuckled. "Don't worry about that. The photographer told me he was quite pleased with you."

"Really?" Cheered, Nicole straightened her aching shoulders. "I'm glad."

"I've had several more calls about you," Alain told her. "That department store ad got a lot of attention; I think you're going to have a full schedule."

Nicole wrinkled her brow. She was pleased about her blossoming career, yet still anxious at the thought of her parents' dismay if she devoted too much time to modeling and not enough to school-work.

Alain seemed to read her thoughts. "Don't worry," he told her. "I know what your parents said. But I can tell you now, when you're out of school, we can get you all the work you want. I think by that time you'll have enough experience for the really top jobs."

Nicole opened her eyes wide. *"Vraiment?"* she asked. "I can't believe it. You really think I'm that good?"

"I'm sure of it, *ma petite*," Alain responded. "Guard your nest egg. New York is an expensive place."

"New York?" Nicole was bewildered. "What about New York?"

"New York's the center of high fashion modeling—in this country, at least. Maybe eventually you'll go to London, Paris, Rome—who knows?"

Nicole thought she must be dreaming. Nicole Lewis—an internationally renowned model? "Alain, you really think so?"

"Who knows?" he repeated, taking a sip of his coffee. "We will see, *ma petite*. Work hard and save your money. And when the time comes, you'll be ready."

"Mon dieu." Nicole gulped down the rest of her coffee, her hunger and cold almost forgotten. She could see it now: Nicole Lewis on the cover of *Vogue* and *Mademoiselle*, breakfast in London and dinner in Paris, bright lights, high fashion, amusing people.

"Call me Monday morning and we'll schedule your next assignment."

Nicole, still lost in her daydream, nodded absently. She would work hard, save her money, leave home. . . . A sudden realization slashed through her thoughts and brought her to her senses. The money she earned was earmarked for her college fund—she and her parents had agreed on that—it was the whole purpose for her part-time modeling. Where did college fit into Alain's plans for her?

Nicole had a sinking feeling that it didn't fit at all.

Chapter 4

"*M*ollie, will you get a move on!" Cindy strapped her books to the back of her bike, then straddled the seat of her beach cruiser.

"I'm coming, I'm coming." Mollie took one last look at herself in the hall mirror, then followed her sister reluctantly out the back door.

Too late, it had occurred to her that telling all her friends about her proposed entry into the world of high fashion hadn't been the greatest idea. The phone calls had started coming Friday evening, and Mollie had been forced to confess her lack of success. So the worst was over, yet she still dreaded facing all her friends at school.

"Me and my big mouth," she grumbled to herself as she wheeled her bike out of the garage. "Cindy, wait up!"

Sure enough, after the girls reached the high school and parked their bikes at the racks, Mollie found Sarah and Linda waiting just inside the doors.

"Cheer up, Mollie," Sarah said after one look at her friend's face. "At least you tried. I wouldn't have had the nerve to do that much."

Mollie tried to smile, but when Linda added, "After all, we can't all look like Nicole," she found it impossible.

"I'm going to spend my whole life feeling inferior to my own sister," Mollie wailed.

Her two friends gazed at her, their sympathy obvious. "I'm glad Nicole's not *my* sister," Linda said. "Having an older sister that's pretty and smart, too, is more than anybody can handle. Come on, Mollie, we'll be late to class. I'll treat you to a sundae after school. Maybe that will cheer you up."

"Why not?" Mollie groaned. "I might as well get fat, since I'll never be a model."

It didn't help that during French I, Mrs. Preston remembered to ask, "How did the big audition go, Mollie?"

"Not too well." Mollie tried to look as if it didn't matter. But it did.

"*Quel dommage,*" the teacher murmured, her tone kind.

Mollie nodded and opened her book to the day's lesson. But who could concentrate on French verbs when her whole life had just been ruined? It's not fair, she told herself once more. Nicole has all the luck!

Mollie was putting her books away before lunch

when someone struck her a hearty blow on the shoulder.

"What—" Mollie looked around to see Heather grinning broadly at her. Oh no, Mollie thought. Another friend trying to cheer me up. Although Heather was a junior, she and Mollie had become friends during the fall play, when Mollie had played the lead role in *Grease*, and Heather had also been in the cast. But Heather wasn't interested in Mollie's nonexistent modeling career.

"You'll never guess!"

"What?" Mollie looked perplexed. She had never seen the chubby girl so excited.

"My cousin called me last night. She saw it in the L.A. paper, but I didn't believe it until I saw it with my own eyes. Come on!"

"Where are we going?" Mollie shouted as Heather dragged her ruthlessly through the crowded hallway.

"The school library. I want you to read this."

The big room held only a few students. Mollie was still protesting loudly when Heather pushed her through the doors. The librarian looked up at them, frowning, and Mollie quickly lowered her voice to a whisper.

"Have you flipped out?"

But when Heather stopped in front of the newspaper rack and pulled out the previous day's edition of *Variety*, thumbing the news sheets until she found the page she sought, Mollie's eyes widened.

A large ad proclaimed: OPEN AUDITION: SEEKING TWO ACTRESSES, AGES 16–18, FOR FEATURE FILM PRODUCTION.

Mollie scanned the rest of the ad, hardly able to believe her eyes. "Are you going to try out?"

"Is the ocean blue?"

"Wow," Mollie murmured, trying to ignore the wave of envy that swept over her. It was bad enough having a sister who was a model. Soon she'd have a friend who was a famous actress, too. And Mollie would be nothing more than a has-been, worse, a never-has-been, living her life through her sister and her friend. This tragic scenario was interrupted by Heather's urgent whisper.

"Don't you want to come, too?"

"Me?" Mollie gulped. "Of course I do. But I'm not sixteen."

"So? Actresses never give their real ages. You know that." Heather shrugged off such a minor detail. "Look, it's in Los Angeles on Saturday, eight A.M. till two P.M."

"L.A.? How will we get there?"

"I passed my driver's test last month, remember?"

"Of course." Mollie could hardly believe her good fortune. "Did you write down the address?"

"Are you kidding? It's engraved on my brain."

But just to be safe, they copied down the street address and the name of the production company. Then Mollie said good-bye to Heather, who was already late to study hall, and headed for the lunch room.

By the time she had made her way through the long line and spotted Sarah and Linda at a table, her two friends were almost finished with their hamburgers.

"What happened to you?" Sarah asked.

Mollie opened her mouth, ready to spill her exciting news, then bit back the impulsive words. What if she didn't get the part? One major embarrassment per week was more than enough. "Heather wanted to tell me something."

"What about?" Linda looked up from her French fries.

"Just a part she wants to try out for."

The two freshmen nodded. Everyone knew that Heather was a devoted actress who never missed participating in any of the school plays. Mollie breathed easier.

"Has Ms. Black selected the spring musical already?"

"No." Mollie took a bite of her cheeseburger. "She hasn't made the final selection, but she's got several possibilities in mind." Which was bound to be true, she thought, concentrating on her sandwich to avoid further questions. She was thankful when the girls' conversation turned to other important matters, such as Sarah's latest date with her boyfriend, Andrew.

The rest of the day was lost in a glorious daydream, as Mollie's imagination painted glowing pictures of her life as a star. "After all," she told herself as she pedaled home from school, "everybody said I did a great job as Sandy in the fall musical."

When she walked into the house, greeted by a rambunctious Winston, she patted the big Newfoundland rather absently, and wandered up to her bedroom, willing the phone to ring. But though it rang twice, both calls were for Nicole, and Mollie began to worry that Heather hadn't been able to get permission to drive to Los Angeles.

It was Mollie's turn to set the table, and she was still so absent-minded that she dropped two forks and broke a plate. She quickly swept up the pieces before anyone could see.

When the family gathered around the table for some of Laura Lewis's savory chicken with rice, the conversation flowed right past Mollie. Her father had to speak to her twice before she looked up with a start.

"What?"

"I asked about your day," her father repeated patiently. "Must have been awfully good or pretty bad. You look like you're in another world tonight."

"Probably some new guy she's in love with." Cindy grinned as she took another helping of chicken. "Who is it this time, Mollie?"

Mollie flushed with embarrassment, murmuring, "That's not it at all." Then, suddenly afraid that they would ask just what *was* on her mind, she stammered, "I mean, not exactly."

They all laughed, and her father gazed at his youngest daughter fondly. "Same old Mollie."

His tone was indulgent, but Mollie felt insulted. Little did they know that they were harboring a future star in their midst. They wouldn't laugh so easily when she was on the cover of *People* magazine.

Determined not to expose her secret ambition prematurely, Mollie looked down at her plate.

"How about you, Cindy? How was school?" Mr.

Lewis looked at his middle daughter, who was putting away a substantial amount of food.

"Great. Swim practice went well, and the biology classes are signing up for a grunion run."

"Sounds thrilling," their mother said, as she handed around the salad. "How do you like my new recipe for vinaigrette dressing, Nicole?"

"Pretty ordinary," was Nicole's answer.

They all stared at her. Nicole, looking up to see their expressions of surprise, turned red. "Did you ask me about my day?"

"Don't tell me Nicole's in love, too?" Cindy hooted. "This whole family's going senile; better watch out, Dad." She stood up, piling her dishes to take into the kitchen, and paused long enough to drop a quick kiss on her father's balding head.

Mollie, intrigued, forgot her own concerns for a moment. Nicole, ever since breaking up with her boyfriend Mark before Christmas, had had plenty of dates, but no one special in her life. "Have you met someone new, Nicole?"

"No, no," her sister said quickly. "I was just daydreaming." She stood up, too, and followed Cindy into the kitchen, hoping to avoid further questions. Alain had already called her with another assignment for the weekend and Nicole hadn't yet broken the news to her parents.

"Nicole," her mother called after her, and Nicole tensed. "Did you mail the housing questionnaires to Smith and Vassar?"

"I forgot," Nicole confessed.

Her mother frowned. "Time's running out, Nicole. You've still got a few college details to complete; you wouldn't want to get left out of the dorms you prefer."

"I know, Mother," Nicole said quickly. "I'll take care of it tomorrow, I promise." She disappeared into the kitchen, and began to scrape dishes with a vigor that made Cindy look at her in surprise.

"What's with you?"

"Nothing." Nicole stacked the dishes into the dishwasher, wishing that her family wouldn't be so nosy. Every time her parents mentioned college lately, Nicole felt as if her modeling ambitions were printed across her forehead for everyone to read. But she wasn't ready to face her parents with an alternate plan. At least, not yet.

Cindy frowned thoughtfully as she went to the pantry to get some cat food. "Be that way," she muttered to the two cats, who followed her eagerly as she took the cans of cat food back to the can opener. "Sisters!"

Cindy looked up at the sound of the telephone, but Mollie, in the dining room, shrieked, "I'll get it!"

Mollie ran to the phone in the hallway and grabbed the receiver. "Hello?"

"Mollie?"

"Yes." Mollie felt excitement building when she recognized Heather's voice. "Did you get permission to drive to L.A.?"

"It took some fast talking, but I did it," Heather answered, sounding triumphant. "I told them we were going to Magic Mountain for the day."

Mollie, who liked amusement parks as much as anyone, was puzzled. "Why?"

"You know parents; they might not like us going into Hollywood alone for the day."

"Good thinking," Mollie agreed, though she felt a stab of dismay that she would have to lie.

As soon as she hung up, Mollie went to find her dad. Mr. Lewis was stretched out on the recliner in the den, hidden behind the evening newspaper.

"Dad?"

"Uhmm?"

"Can I go to L.A. with Heather on Saturday? She wants to go to Magic Mountain."

Richard Lewis lowered his paper and peered through his glasses at his youngest daughter. "And what kind of driver is she?"

"Super safe, Dad. Honest. She drove to the drama club caroling party before Christmas, remember? You liked her, didn't you?"

Mr. Lewis appeared to consider. "Yes, she seems like a mature young lady. I suppose it's all right, as long as you're home before dark."

"Hooray! Thanks, Dad." Mollie, feeling like a real sneak, gave her dad a quick hug, then ran upstairs before her excitement could give her away. A real audition! How could she live until Saturday?

The week crawled by with agonizing slowness, but eventually Saturday dawned, overcast and gray. Nicole, drinking a cup of creamy French coffee at the breakfast table, peered at the gloomy skies outside the window and felt thankful that today she was shooting indoors.

Mollie came through the swinging door and

grabbed a croissant from the tray. "Delicious," she said, taking a bite. "Modeling again?"

Nicole nodded, afraid that her youngest sister might not like being reminded of her recent failure. But to Nicole's surprise, Mollie's thoughts seemed far away.

"That's nice." Mollie ladled on a generous helping of strawberry jam and gobbled down the rest of the flaky pastry.

Nicole looked at her more closely, inspecting her sister's elaborate hairdo and heavy makeup.

"What are you up to?"

"Oh, I'm going to Magic Mountain with Heather."

"In that outfit? In the rain?"

Nicole sounded suspicious, so Mollie answered quickly, "It may not rain, after all." Just then the sound of a car horn saved Mollie from further interrogation. "There's Heather. See you."

She grabbed a jacket and ran out to the driveway, pulling open the door of the red sedan and climbing in beside her friend. "Let's go!"

The drive to Los Angeles was uneventful. Heather concentrated on the road, and Mollie lost herself in blissful daydreams, all centering on a certain Lewis sister's meteoric rise to fame.

When they located the correct street and, with more difficulty, at last found a parking space, Mollie felt her stomach begin to knot with nervousness. She wished she had ignored those croissants, which no longer seemed so light and flaky.

But Heather immediately climbed out of the car and urged Mollie to follow her.

As they turned a corner, nearing the big build-

ing that had been listed in the ad, Heather came
to an abrupt stop. Mollie, following close behind,
walked straight into her.

"Ugh," Heather gasped.

"I'm sorry, but you shouldn't stop like that,"
Mollie told her.

"I didn't mean you. Look at that line!"

Mollie's mouth dropped open.

Girls of all shapes and sizes, with a smattering
of mothers and other adults, formed a line that
snaked around the long building and into the
alley.

"This is awful!"

Heather shrugged. "I guess we should have expected it. Everybody wants to be an actress."

The two girls hurried to take their place in the
line before it could get even longer, and stood
behind two girls with blue-streaked hair and wild
outfits that Mollie examined with interest.

"Look at that green knit tunic," she whispered
to her friend.

Heather, who was trying to avoid the garbage
that littered the alley from an overturned trash
can, wrinkled her nose in disgust. "What? Oh,
that. Forget it, Mollie, you'd look like an overripe
avocado if you wore that."

"Thanks a bunch," Mollie snapped. "What time
is it?"

"Five after eight."

"Maybe the line will start to move soon."

"The eternal optimist," Heather sighed. "We'll
see."

They leaned against the faded brick wall and

waited. The line did begin to inch forward, but with painful slowness. Mollie had worn her tightest, trendiest shoes, and now her feet hurt.

"Look at the girls with the lawn chairs, Heather. That's what we should have brought."

"Now you tell me," Heather complained. "I think we should have packed a lunch. I'm *starved*."

"At the rate this line is moving, we'll probably miss dinner, too." Even Mollie was beginning to feel downcast.

By the time they had worked their way around the corner, more than an hour had passed and girls continued to arrive, swelling the line past any semblance of order.

"Hey, we were here first," Heather yelled, when one girl in an outrageous purple sweater tried to push in front of them. The girl, who looked much older than eighteen, simply sneered.

"Who cares?"

"You'd better!" Heather's face flushed with anger, and Mollie looked at them both in alarm, afraid the stranger would resort to actual blows.

The girls in front of them turned to stare, and there were several shouts of "Stop pushing," and "We were here first!"

A man in a business suit walked down the line, and the crowd quieted to hear him. "If we don't have order here, I'll close the auditions right now, and you can all go home!"

Mollie swallowed and looked anxiously at Heather. Her friend's belligerence faded, and she gave one last hard look at the encroaching stranger, who sullenly took her place behind the two Santa Barbara girls.

Mollie breathed easier and the line continued to shuffle forward.

"What time is it?" she asked some time later, sure that the day must be almost over.

"Twelve-thirty," Heather told her glumly. "I'm about to expire from hunger!"

"Me, too," Mollie admitted. "I hope they don't close the auditions before we even get to the door."

"Don't even think it," Heather frowned. "What else can happen to us today?"

Mollie sighed, feeling a suspicious drop touch her face. "You shouldn't have said that."

The overcast sky at last fulfilled its implicit promise; a light but steady rain began to fall. There were cries of dismay all along the line, and the girl in front of them with the blue hair began to develop blue streaks down her cheeks. That was such a funny sight that Mollie almost forgot her own despair over the ruin of her careful hairdo.

"Let's hope they're auditioning for *Singing in the Rain*," Heather quipped.

They both laughed, then scrunched up as close to the wall of the building as they could, shivering inside their jackets, and shifting back and forth on aching legs.

Another eternity passed before the entrance to the large hall at last came into view. Mollie, thoroughly soaked now and chilled to the bone, let out a hopeful sigh.

"Heather, I can actually see a man at a desk inside the doorway."

"It's past two, pray that they don't close before we get inside."

Mollie crossed all her fingers; her toes were too numb to feel or she would have tried to cross them, too. The line continued to crawl forward.

As they slowly approached their goal, Mollie began to forget her weariness in a new rush of nervousness. She had rehearsed all week: her credits in school plays, her eagerness for the role, her willingness to work hard and learn any new skills, anything that she had thought might impress a casting director. Now her whole carefully prepared speech flew out of her head like an errant butterfly escaping a collector's net. They stepped across the threshold into a big barn of a building, and she stared at the man behind the desk, her mind completely blank.

"Name?"

"Uh—" Heather nudged her, not very gently, and Mollie tried to pull herself together. "Mollie Lewis."

"Heather Wynn-Sommers," her friend said.

The man looked up at them for the first time. He looked tired. His eyes were red, as if he had stared at too many applications today. Mollie, conscious of wet hair straggling around her face and makeup ruined by the long damp wait, tried not to cringe.

The man shook his head. "Sorry, girls; not this time."

"What do you mean?" Mollie said.

"Don't we even get to read for the part?" Heather protested.

"We're looking for completely different types. Sorry." His tone was final.

Heather, always self-conscious about her weight, assumed he meant thinner girls, and Mollie, wishing for some magic potion that would induce instant growth, gritted her teeth. They had no choice but to step out of line and allow the girls pushing eagerly behind them to step forward.

Outside in the rain once more, Mollie looked at Heather, and knew that her friend's expression of chagrin was mirrored on her own face.

"All that time we waited, and he turned us down in thirty seconds!"

"We should have brought Nicole," Heather groaned. "I bet she's the type he wanted."

"Shut up!" Mollie wailed.

Chapter 5

$\mathcal{M}$ollie wanted nothing more than to slip into the house unnoticed, so she was dismayed to find a reception committee waiting when she got home. Laura Lewis pounced on her youngest daughter as soon as Mollie walked through the front door.

"I knew it." Mrs. Lewis shook her head. "Mollie, you're soaked. You'll probably catch pneumonia. Here, don't drip on the carpet."

"I'm fine, Mom," Mollie protested, ruining the effect by sneezing loudly.

Nicole looked out of the kitchen, a spatula in her hand, and Cindy, who had been wrestling with Winston, got up from the floor.

"You look like a drowned rat, Mollie," Nicole said, then disappeared back into the kitchen.

"I was worried about you girls driving in the rain on those slick freeways. There are always so many accidents in this weather." Laura Lewis continued to fuss, and Mollie sneezed again.

"Watch it, shrimp," Cindy warned. "Don't get your germs on Winston."

"Go upstairs right now and get out of those wet clothes. Then take a hot shower and I'll fix you some soup," Mrs. Lewis said.

"Oh, Mom." Mollie shook her head at her mother, but headed for the stairs anyway. After she pulled off her wet clothes and took a quick shower, she crawled into bed, pulling the thick comforter over her and delighting in the warmth that slowly returned to her weary body.

Laura Lewis appeared in the doorway with a tray for Mollie. A savory aroma wafted from a bowl of chicken soup, blending with the spicy fragrance of a mug of steaming tea. Mrs. Lewis set the tray on the bed, smoothed the rumpled sheets, and bent to give Mollie a light kiss.

Mollie took a sip of the hot spiced tea, her depression beginning to lift. Sometimes a little mothering wasn't such a bad thing, even for a mature fourteen-year-old.

"Feeling better?"

Mollie nodded. "Thanks for the soup. It smells delicious."

"You're welcome. I've got to get back to the kitchen. I'm testing a new crepe recipe."

"Yumm," Mollie said. "Save me some."

"I will," her mother promised.

Mollie finished off the soup quickly and sipped the rest of her tea. She pushed back the tray, but the soft cocoon of bedcoverings was too comfortable to leave, especially when Cinders came into her room and jumped up on the bed. He curled up beside her into a contented ball and began to purr. Mollie stroked his mottled gray fur, wishing it would take that little to make her happy. Her expression was so pensive that when Nicole came into the room carrying a dish of delicious crepes, she frowned at her little sister.

"Are you really sick, Mollie?"

Mollie brightened at the sight of the golden crepes dusted with powdered sugar and stuffed with fresh peaches. She managed a brave smile and said, "I'm okay. I'm thinking of becoming a social worker."

"Really?" Nicole looked startled. "Why?"

"Oh, I don't know." Mollie attacked the dessert with zest. "I think it would be nice to give up all worldly delights and devote myself to the poor."

Nicole tried not to smile as she watched her sister lick her lips in order not to miss one speck of sugar, and asked gravely, "What brought on this attack of social zeal?"

"I'm obviously not cut out to be a success at anything spectacular," Mollie told her. "I might as well do something to help the world."

Nicole sat down on the side of the bed and regarded her younger sister intently. "This sudden soul-searching is not the result of a trip to Magic Mountain, even if you did get wet and tired. What happened, Mollie?"

"Nothing." But Mollie felt her face growing pink under her sister's steady gaze, and the desire to tell someone her troubles became too strong to resist.

"You won't tell Mom?"

"Not unless it's something really terrible," Nicole promised cautiously. "You haven't flunked out of school?"

"Of course not; how could I manage that on a Saturday?" Mollie demanded.

"Well, what then?"

"I'm a failure, Nicole."

"Oh, Mollie." Nicole felt a pang of guilt: she was doing so well with her modeling assignments; today again Alain had hinted at a bright future in store for her. Poor little Mollie. Nicole sometimes wanted to strangle her, but after all Mollie was her sister and she was obviously still dejected over Alain's negative assessment of her as a model. Nicole shook her head.

"Just because you didn't get the chance to model—"

"It's worse than that." Mollie sounded truly tragic, and Nicole paused, apprehension making her voice stern.

"Mollie, what have you done?"

"Heather and I tried to audition for a part in a movie," Mollie admitted in a small voice.

Nicole sighed in relief. "And?"

"Neither of us got a part. They wouldn't even let us read. They said they were looking for different types—probably someone just like you." The gloom in Mollie's voice would have been funny if it hadn't been so obviously heartfelt. "I'm a failure," she repeated, tears forming in her huge blue eyes.

Nicole reached out to shake her sister gently.

"You dodo; how many other girls got turned down at the audition?"

"Hundreds."

"Doesn't that tell you something? It's not you, Mollie. You're cute and sweet, and you did a good job in the fall musical. Just because you didn't take Hollywood by storm doesn't mean you're a failure. Think about all your successes!"

Mollie tried to catch some of Nicole's positive spirit, but she still felt like a loser. Sighing, she said, "Don't tell Mom and Dad."

"I won't." Nicole, uneasily aware that she had her own secrets—how could she tell her parents that Alain thought she should model full time? —changed the subject abruptly.

"You probably wouldn't even *enjoy* acting professionally, Mollie."

"I had a great time doing *Grease*," Mollie told her indignantly. And she had too, at least after she got over her panic at having to kiss a boy in front of a live audience. To a girl who'd never been kissed before, it had been pretty traumatic— especially when she couldn't even confess to her friends, who thought she was more experienced, why she was so worried. But Mollie had almost forgotten that minor detail. Her voice was emphatic now as she argued her point.

"That was different," Nicole insisted. "You didn't have to devote your whole life to the play."

"But Nicole, it would be so exciting to be a real actress. You've got something glamorous and interesting to do, and I'm stuck in the same old rut. It isn't fair!"

Nicole looked at her sister thoughtfully. "Mollie, even modeling isn't as much fun as you think it is." She rubbed her neck absently. It still ached from holding her head at the same angle for minutes at a time during the morning's shoot. "It's hard work, actually."

Mollie looked unconvinced. Nicole had a sudden idea.

"If I can get permission, would you like to go on a shoot with me? You can get a better idea of what I really do, and I don't think you'll envy me quite as much."

Mollie sat up in bed abruptly, almost overturning the dishes on the tray. "Oh, Nicole, you mean it? Really?"

"You'll probably get bored before we're done," Nicole told her wryly, "but I'll see what I can do, okay?"

"Great!"

Chapter 6

*W*hen Nicole and Mollie set out together the following Saturday, Mollie was bursting with excitement. True, it was Nicole who would be doing the modeling, but at least Mollie could catch a glimpse of what went on behind the cameras.

"This will give me something to write that essay about for English," she told Nicole. "Thanks for getting me off the hook."

"Next time . . ." Nicole began, slipping into her big sister tone of voice.

"I know, I know," Mollie grumbled. "Don't open my big mouth before I know for sure what's going to happen."

"Right."

But even that admonition didn't dim Mollie's sense of anticipation. Somewhere in the back of her mind, a tiny hope still burned that someone at the modeling session might just notice that there was another Lewis sister with certain claims to grace and beauty. So Mollie sat on the bus beside her sister and dreamed blissful daydreams.

When they got off the bus and made their way down the sidewalk to the studio, Mollie had to walk quickly to stay beside her taller sister.

"Aren't you nervous?" Mollie asked, trying not to feel envious of Nicole, who appeared so serene and cool as she strode along.

"Not really," Nicole answered. "With each assignment I do, the more prepared I feel."

She sounded so confident and assured that Mollie looked at her sister with new respect.

"You have to be very quiet and stay out of everybody's way, Mollie. I had to do a lot of fast talking to get you in, so don't let me down."

"I'll be as quiet as a mouse, I promise," Mollie said earnestly.

They turned into the building and took the elevator to the third floor. Nicole led the way into the big studio and headed straight for the dressing room.

Mollie, following her sister meekly, looked at the long mirrors and bright lights, the tubes and jars of cosmetics that littered the counter. She suppressed a sharp pang of envy. She would love to experiment with all that makeup. But, remembering her promise to Nicole, she resisted her urge to pick up the nearest container, and instead stood back against the wall and watched a makeup artist go to work on Nicole's face.

"Hi, Nicole," another girl said. "There's no rush. The photographer hasn't shown up yet."

"Hi, Gina. What happened?"

"I have no idea. The crew is having a fit and the art director's been on the phone for thirty minutes trying to locate him."

Nevertheless, the makeup artist continued to apply Nicole's makeup with a practiced hand. "When he does get here, they'll be in even more of a rush than usual," she warned the auburn-haired model.

Gina laughed. "You're right," she agreed. As she turned away, she caught a glimpse of Mollie in the mirror. "Who's the kid?"

"Oh, sorry. Gina, this is my sister, Mollie."

"Hi, Mollie."

"Hello." Mollie's reply was stiff. She didn't appreciate being called a kid.

"She's doing a report on modeling for school." Nicole sounded almost defensive, and Mollie began to feel distinctly *de trop*, as Nicole would have said. She moved even further into the corner and tried to make herself as small as possible.

Two more girls hurried into the dressing room, and soon the small room seemed to overflow with people. Mollie watched the girls become even more gorgeous as the makeup artists perfected their already beautiful faces, and the hairdressers created glamorous styles for their hair. Then the models began to try on the clothes that hung along the back wall. How she longed to be one of them! Mollie sighed, but no one noticed. The noisy chatter of the girls in front of the mirror quieted only when the art director put his head in the door and said, "Okay, girls. We're ready to start."

"Did the photographer finally show up?" one of the other girls asked.

"Jim? No, he had an argument with a cattle truck on the freeway this morning, and his VW came out second best."

The girls gasped. "Is he okay?" Gina asked.

"Broken leg." The man shook his head. "He would have to do this the day we're shooting. I had to call half the photographers in L.A. to find someone to come in on such short notice."

Mollie waited until the girls filed out, then followed silently behind them, trying to find a good vantage point where she could watch what was happening without getting in the way.

That was harder than it first appeared: the studio was littered with cables and wires and there seemed to be lots of stray scenery lying around for use in later shooting. Mollie finally perched herself on a somewhat unsteady stool in front of a large table stacked with tubs of margarine—props for the next shoot—and watched the photographer placing the models in their assigned positions.

It seemed to take ages for the man to get the girls in exactly the right spot. Then the photographer changed his mind and decided to rearrange the whole set up. Meanwhile, the models waited patiently.

Mollie was beginning to see why Nicole came home so tired after these sessions.

At last the girls were regrouped one more time,

then the photographer and his assistant rearranged some of the big lights, and they began to take pictures. A few shots later, all the girls ran to change clothes—and the whole thing started over again.

Mollie shifted on her stool. She hated to admit that Nicole was right, but she was beginning to get bored. She glanced at her watch—only half past eleven—she could have sworn they had been at this all day. Did models get to eat lunch?

She shifted her weight again on the rickety little stool, and heard an ominous crack. The back leg of the stool gave way, and she slid backward into the table. The table tilted under the sudden weight, and the whole pyramid of margarine tubs went flying in a dozen different directions. The sound of multiple crashes seemed to echo endlessly in the big studio, as Mollie finally hit the floor with a resounding wallop.

For a moment the room swam around her, and she blinked, gulping from the impact of the unexpected fall. As she looked up, as one last plastic tub came tumbling down onto her head, she realized with horror that the whole roomful of people had rushed to see what had happened.

"What are you doing, trying to wreck the place?" the art director demanded. "What's this kid doing here?"

Nicole, standing just behind the man, was white with shock and embarrassment. Mollie, her own face hot and red in mortification, wished that she could crawl into a mouse hole.

"That's my sister. I—we—" Nicole seemed at a

loss for words. The man had apparently forgotten that she had asked permission to bring her sister along to watch.

Mollie fought back tears of chagrin; Nicole would never, never forgive her for making a fool of her in front of all her new colleagues. Mollie swallowed hard to hold back the tears, staring resolutely at the floor.

Someone started to laugh. Mollie, torn between indignation and relief, looked up to see the photographer beginning to chuckle. Nicole watched him anxiously, looking from him to the art director, and her tense expression relaxed just a little as the other man also began to grin. The other models dissolved into a chorus of giggles.

Mollie, willing to accept the laughter with good grace as long as nobody got angry at Nicole for having brought her, gave a wobbly smile. "I'm really sorry; I didn't mean to do it."

"Good thing we weren't filming bowling balls later today; you'd have demolished the whole building." The art director shook his head at her. "Try not to knock anything else over until we're through, okay?"

"I won't," Mollie said, so relieved to see his gruffness disarmed that she would have willingly agreed to wait down in the lobby. But although the rest of the staff started back to finish the session, the photographer continued to stare at her.

Mollie, wondering if she had margarine on her face, tried unobtrusively to rub her nose.

"I must look like an underdone English muffin," she moaned.

The man chuckled again. "You're pretty funny, kid," he said.

"Really?" The remark seemed intended as a compliment, so Mollie didn't bristle, but she was puzzled.

"As a matter of fact . . ." He hesitated, but continued to stare at her until Mollie was certain there was something wrong with her face. "Have you done any acting?"

"A little," Mollie told him, and then wondered if school plays were what he had in mind.

But he seemed to come to a decision, because he reached inside his back pocket and pulled out a business card, writing something on the back before handing it to Mollie.

"My girlfriend's company is looking for a teen-ager for a pilot for a new sitcom. I think you're just the type she needs. If you go to this address Tuesday at nine and give them my card, I'll tell her to watch for you. She might decide to have you do a reading."

Mollie's eyes widened, and she gasped—more stunned by this unexpected good fortune than she had been by the fall.

"Gosh," she murmured. "Thank you!"

But the man had already turned back to the waiting models, and Mollie was left behind to sit carefully on the hard floor—no more unreliable seats today—and lose herself in a whole new set of splendid daydreams. A sitcom! Who could have imagined that!

With so much to think about, Mollie didn't begrudge the tedium of the rest of the shoot.

Nicole wished fervently for the shoot to end. Her back ached and she was getting a super headache, either from staring into the bright lights or from the shock of seeing her little sister turning the studio upside down. It didn't help that halfway through the art director suddenly decided that he didn't like her hairstyle.

"Hey, you in the blue," he called.

Nicole, who was wearing a powder blue outfit, jumped. "Yes?"

"Go tell the stylist to do something more interesting with your hair; it's really too boring."

Nicole, who had asked the hair stylist for one of her favorite styles, a simple but elegant French roll, looked guilty.

Gina, the auburn-haired girl who was standing beside her in a mint-green outfit, murmured, "Don't look so upset, Nicole."

Nicole threw her a grateful glance, then hurried back to repeat the instructions to the stylist. The hairstylist, who looked slightly irritated, began to rearrange her hair. Nicole winced as the comb poked her sensitive scalp.

When she returned to the set, the photographer waved her back into the picture and they finished the shoot without any more disparaging comments. When the last picture was finally shot, the models walked wearily back to the dressing room to take off their makeup and put on their own clothes. Nicole felt vaguely depressed, as if the photographer's criticism had been personal.

"What's wrong, Nicole?" one of the other girls asked as Nicole sat down in front of the big mirror. "You don't look very happy."

"Mr. Cooper said I was boring."

Further down the counter, Gina laughed. "That's nothing, hon. Wait till they want you to change the *color* of your hair. One year I switched from blond to brunette to red. I was beginning to forget which shade was really mine!"

The other girls giggled at Gina's remark, but Nicole stared at herself in the mirror, trying to imagine herself as a blonde or a redhead. *Mon dieu,* she thought. What next?

In her abstraction, Nicole had almost forgotten about her sister. But when she came out of the dressing room, her tote bag over her arm, she found Mollie waiting quietly outside the door.

"Oh, Mollie!" The memory of the younger girl's embarrassing accident flashed back into Nicole's mind, and she frowned at her sister. "How could you?"

"I didn't mean to, Nicole," Mollie answered meekly. "I'll never do it again."

"*Assurement,*" Nicole murmured, promising herself that she would never again do anything as rash as allowing Mollie near an assignment. If she did, her own budding career might die a quick death.

"I'm really sorry I made a scene in front of all your friends. But it was worth the embarrassment. I think I've been discovered!" Mollie chattered away as she followed Nicole out of the studio and toward the elevator, scurrying like an anxious puppy to keep up with the taller girl's longer strides.

"What?"

"You know, like Lana Turner, that movie star who was drinking a soda at the right drugstore. That guy, he gave me his card."

"*Comment?* What are you talking about?" Nicole pushed the elevator button and turned to stare at her sister in surprise.

"The photographer," Mollie sighed, still ecstatic over her unexpected good fortune. "He says I may be just right for a new sitcom! I'm going to be on television, Nicole!"

"*Mon dieu!*" Nicole said, ignoring the open elevator door as she gazed at Mollie in horror. What had she started now?

Chapter 7

"*T*elevision?" Laura Lewis frowned at her youngest daughter. "Mollie, if this is one of your wild schemes—"

"He said I was perfect for the part," Mollie argued indignantly. "Well, he almost said that. Anyhow, he said I might get to read for it. Isn't it the most exciting thing you ever heard?"

Her mother looked so perturbed that Cindy, who had just wandered into the kitchen and saw her mother and Nicole staring anxiously at the youngest Lewis, pushed aside the earphones of her Walkman to inquire, "Is Mollie in trouble? What'd she do?"

"Nothing," Mollie snapped. "But I'm going to be a television star."

"You and Lassie," Cindy chortled, overcome with laughter at such a ridiculous idea. But when she saw that neither her mother nor Nicole joined in, she sobered. "Is she serious?"

"I'm afraid so," Mrs. Lewis said.

"What is everybody looking so grim about?" Mollie demanded. "This is my big chance! Aren't you happy for me?"

She looked at the other members of her family, her excitement dimmed by this unexpected reception of her big news. "Nicole is working, and making money, and getting lots of attention. Nobody made a big fuss about that. Don't you want me to be successful, too?"

Her tone was so plaintive that Nicole flushed, looking guilty. "It's not that we don't want you to have your share of the limelight, Mollie, believe me. I'd be delighted to see you become famous—if it made you happy."

"Why shouldn't it?" Mollie's expression was perplexed.

Nicole looked at her mother. Mrs. Lewis sighed and put one arm around her youngest daughter. "Mollie, show business is a difficult way of life even for an adult, very demanding and very stressful. It can be destructive to your self esteem and sometimes even to your value system. And if it's a turbulent way of life for grown-ups, think how much more difficult it can be for children. It's certainly not the kind of life your father and I ever imagined for you."

"But I'm not a child; I'm fourteen," Mollie wailed. "You can't refuse to let me try! I may never get another chance like this. You said I was good in the fall play. _Everyone_ said so. I'm a great actress."

Cindy rolled her eyes, but Mollie ignored her.

"At least, I could be. How will I know if I never try?"

Laura Lewis, observing the stubborn set of Mollie's round chin, sighed. "I'll talk to your father, and then we'll see, dear."

Mollie, only slightly placated, stalked out of the kitchen and up to her room to bemoan the harshness of her fate to whichever of the animals would listen.

The others watched her go, and Cindy pulled her earphones back into place. "Don't worry, Mom," she said blithely, "let her go to the audition; she'll never make it anyhow. There'll be lots of experienced actresses trying out for the part."

"But what if she *does* get the part?" Mrs. Lewis murmured. She and Nicole exchanged worried glances.

Mollie curled up on her bed, contemplating the unfairness of life in general, and the particular unfairness of her own situation. Couldn't her mother and father see what a great opportunity this was? How could they possibly think of denying Mollie her big chance?

"If it were Nicole who had been asked to audition, they wouldn't hesitate," Mollie told Cinders, stroking the soft fur as the lanky cat purred contentedly. "Just because I'm the youngest, they always think I can't handle a new situation. Talk about favoritism!"

She didn't come out of her room until Cindy came to call her to dinner.

"Soup's on, shrimp," she said, pausing at the sight of Mollie's gloomy expression. "You're really make a big deal over nothing, you know."

"It's not nothing," Mollie began hotly. "This is my big chance!"

"That's not what I meant. They haven't even said no yet—why don't you wait till they turn you down before you turn into a sad sack? You always go off the deep end, shrimp. That's *exactly* what Mom and Dad are worried about. Pouting in your room is hardly the way to show them how grown-up you are."

Mollie made a face at her sister, who simply shrugged and left the room. But after Cindy had gone, Mollie reluctantly came to the conclusion that her sister was probably right. She went down to dinner with a smile pasted on her face, determined to act more cheerful.

But the meal was still a rather quiet one, and Mollie couldn't resist throwing inquisitive glances at her mother and father whenever she thought they weren't looking. After everyone had finished, Mrs. Lewis left the girls to clear away the dishes and she and her husband went into the den.

Mollie could hardly bear the suspense. She knew they were discussing her. What were they saying?

"Hurry up with those dishes," Cindy complained. "I want to get out of here, shrimp."

Mollie absent-mindedly grabbed a couple of plates and unintentionally sent a fork flying across the room. It hit the wall with a sharp thump and Nicole winced.

"Careful!"

"I'm sorry," Mollie said. She stacked the plates on the kitchen counter and went back to retrieve the fork. Nicole looked at her narrowly.

"I'm not sure it's safe to let you into the kitchen tonight."

"Oh, Nicole," Mollie wailed. "They've just got to let me try for this part. Do you think they will?"

"I don't know, Mol," Nicole told her sister. At least she was more sympathetic than Cindy had been. "Just remember—"

A step in the hall made her pause, and Mrs. Lewis said from the doorway, "Mollie, come into the den, please."

Mollie, feeling as anxious as if she were being summoned to the guillotine, dropped the sponge she was holding and followed her mother silently back to the den. She found her father sitting in his favorite chair, looking unusually serious. Laura Lewis sat down on the flowered sofa, and Mollie perched nervously on the sofa arm.

"Mollie," her father began, "your mother tells me that you may have the opportunity to try out for a role for a television series."

Mollie nodded, afraid to trust her voice.

"We understand your excitement. I know it sounds very enticing, especially since you've already had a taste of amateur theatrics. But professional acting is really a different story. Have you thought about the changes you'd have to make in your life?"

"Yes." Mollie nodded vigorously, then added, "What changes?"

Her parents exchanged a glance. "If you should get the part and end up in a series, you wouldn't be able to attend school."

"Oh, that." Mollie sounded relieved. "I don't mind."

Richard Lewis's grave expression relaxed somewhat and there was the hint of a twinkle in his blue eyes as he continued.

"You might not mind that sacrifice, but we would, Mollie. Seriously, you'd still have to do your schoolwork. If you were acting steadily, you'd have a special tutor, I believe. But even to take time to audition, we'll have to talk to the school about missing class. And I can tell you right now that your mother and I will only permit this if you agree to make up all the schoolwork you miss. That's going to be a heavy load for you to carry."

"I can do it, Dad, honest," Mollie said earnestly, forgetting for the moment that she was not always the most determined of scholars.

"What about your friends? There'll be little time for parties, movies, ball games—all the fun times at school and afterwards. You'll be a working woman, and that may be more than you're bargaining for."

"Just let me try, Dad, please!"

Mr. Lewis rubbed his balding head. "Another thing—I don't know all the specifics, but I believe that an actor under sixteen requires a chaperon on the set. Your mother and I both have demanding careers of our own. One of us would have to take time from our work to be on the set with you."

Mollie looked perplexed. It hadn't occurred to her that her parents would have to rearrange their schedules, make sacrifices for her. She bit her lip, feeling a twinge of guilt.

"I didn't know that."

Richard Lewis exchanged glances with his wife, then smiled a bit wryly at his daughter. "With all this in mind, Mollie, we have also taken into consideration that you may have a genuine talent. If this is what you really want—we feel that you should have the opportunity to make the attempt. So we're going to let you audition, and then we'll see."

Mollie, whose hopes had been ebbing steadily throughout Mr. Lewis's speech, was taken by surprise. She jumped up and hugged her father, then her mother.

"Thank you, a million trillion times," she exclaimed, dancing around the room. "I think you're the best parents in the world."

Richard Lewis, removing his glasses to rub off the smudges left by Mollie's impulsive embrace, raised his brows slightly. "I just hope we've made the right decision," he said. Laura Lewis sighed and nodded, but Mollie—gloriously happy—didn't even notice.

On Monday Mrs. Lewis made a trip to Vista High for a conference with the principal and counselor. On the condition that Mollie make up all of the work she missed, she received permission to take time off from school.

Mollie went back to class feeling like the luckiest girl in the world, and found Sarah and Linda regarding her with considerable envy.

"I want to hear every single detail when you get back," Sarah told Mollie during study hall.

"I may not get the part," Mollie reminded them, trying to be more realistic this time.

"You will." Linda's voice was gloomy. "I've got a feeling about this, Mollie."

"You don't sound very happy for me," Mollie protested.

"You'll be famous, and we'll never see you again," the other girl told her.

"Of course you will," Mollie argued. "Even if I were famous, I wouldn't forget my friends!"

"When you have your mansion in Beverly Hills, will you invite us to all your parties?" Sarah asked.

"Cross my heart," Mollie told them solemnly. All three girls dissolved into laughter, until the teacher in front of the room called them to order. Still giggling, they tried with little success to turn their minds to such mundane matters as algebra problems and French verbs.

Monday evening Mollie went through her entire wardrobe three times, trying to decide what to wear for the audition. Nicole found her staring at the clothes heaped in great piles around her room.

"Planning a garage sale?"

"Oh, Nicole, I don't know what to wear."

"Wear something you look good in, but something that's comfortable too," Nicole advised.

"But none of these outfits look right," Mollie complained. "Could I borrow your new sweater, please?"

"After what you did to the last sweater you

borrowed from me?" Nicole shook her head. "No way, Mol."

"Darn." Mollie went back to her piles of clothes, trying to make a decision.

"And you'd better clean this room up before Mother sees it, or you may not go anywhere tomorrow," Nicole warned, heading for her own room.

With that kind of motivation, Mollie had her room in an unusual state of order before she went to bed. But she was too nervous to sleep. After an hour of tossing, she got up and went downstairs for a glass of milk.

"I'm scared to death, Winnie," she whispered to the big dog lying on the welcome mat at the back door. He lifted a shaggy head and licked her hand. "At least you believe in me, right?"

When Mollie went back to bed, fortified by cookies and milk, Cinders joined her. At last Mollie fell asleep, stroking the cat and listening to the soft purring.

When her alarm went off the next morning Mollie stirred sleepily, but when she realized what day it was, she sat straight up in bed.

"Oh, no," Mollie moaned. "This is it!" She took her shower in record time, spent as long as she dared on her hair, and put on as much makeup as she thought she could get past her mother's watchful eye.

"Don't you want some breakfast, Mollie?" her mother called from the bottom of the stairs.

"I'm too nervous to eat," Mollie answered, giving her hair one last flip with the brush. "How do I look?"

Nicole, her arms full of school books, paused at the top of the stairs. "You look great, Mollie. Break a leg."

"Don't tell her that," Cindy said from behind them. "Knowing Mollie, she might do it!"

Mollie stuck out her tongue at her middle sister, who only grinned. "Good luck, shrimp."

"Thanks." Mollie took one more look in the mirror, then picked up a jacket and hurried downstairs.

She was so quiet on the drive to Los Angeles that Mrs. Lewis looked at her anxiously more than once. "Are you all right, Mollie? Not having second thoughts?"

"Oh, no," Mollie assured her. "Just about to die of nervousness."

Mrs. Lewis smiled. "Just do your best, Mollie. And don't take it too hard if you don't make it."

"If I just get the chance to try," Mollie sighed.

By the time they parked the car and entered the building, the butterflies in Mollie's stomach were approaching the size of elephants. The woman sitting behind the desk looked so haughty that Mollie fully expected her film career to end right there. But when she presented the business card and personal note from the photographer, the woman looked at her seriously.

"Let me check with Ms. Gardener." She spoke briefly into the phone, then nodded. "Down the hall, second door on the right."

Mollie could hardly believe it. She'd made it

past the front door! She followed her mother across the beige carpet, and into the inner room.

The casting director turned out to be a petite woman with a wild mane of dark hair. Mollie, encouraged to see that this woman was tiny, smiled with more spirit as Mrs. Lewis introduced herself and her daughter.

"Yes, I remember," Ms. Gardener nodded. "We'll give you the chance to read this morning, Mollie. But we do have a lot of young ladies to see today, so don't expect too much."

"Thank you, I won't," Mollie managed to gasp, hardly able to believe her good fortune. She and her mother were directed to another waiting room where a whole crowd of girls waited with parents and other adults in tow. Mollie took a seat beside her mother and looked around at the rest of the group, wondering if they felt as nervous as she did.

Probably so, Mollie decided, watching one cute blonde chewing on a fingernail, and another honey blonde with adorable dimples fingering a button on her blouse until it fell off in her hands. The girl looked so startled that Mollie giggled.

At the other girl's blank stare, Mollie blushed. "I didn't mean—"

"It's okay," the girl grinned. "When I'm nervous, I don't even know I'm doing that. My name's Roberta."

"Mollie Lewis," Mollie told her. "Have you done this a lot?"

"I've done some commercials," Roberta told

her. "Nothing big like this, though. I'm really scared."

"Me, too," Mollie agreed fervently, not willing to admit that she lacked even that much experience. "What do we do now?"

"Wait, mostly." The other girl grimaced. "When they call your name, you get to go in and read for about ten minutes. If they like you, they'll call you back for a second reading."

I hope they like me, Mollie told herself, looking around the room and knowing that every girl there was wishing for the same good fortune.

The inner door opened, and a tall, thin woman called, "Roberta Enderly."

"Oh gosh, that's me," Roberta said. She stood and, followed by a rather anxious-looking woman, started toward the door.

Mollie continued to wait. The minutes crawled by, and each time the door opened, she tensed, waiting to hear which name would be called.

"This is worse than waiting to see the dentist," she whispered to her mother. Mrs. Lewis smiled in sympathy.

The door opened again, and the tall woman said, "Mollie Lewis?"

"Oh, no!" Mollie gulped.

Chapter 8

*M*ollie found herself in a large, rectangular room. At one end several people sat behind a long table. The young woman who had ushered them inside showed Mrs. Lewis to a chair in the back of the room, then motioned Mollie forward.

She pointed to a chair at the side of the room toward the front. "Wait there. They'll be with you in a minute." She handed Mollie a thin sheaf of papers. "Look over the script. You'll be reading a few pages from this."

At Mollie's wide-eyed glance, the woman added, "You don't have to memorize it. Just read it over to familiarize yourself with the lines."

Mollie sat down gingerly on the folding chair—remembering her accident at Nicole's modeling session—and quickly read over the portion of the script she'd been given. It didn't look too difficult.

She glanced up at the men and women behind

the table. She guessed that the important-looking man with a beard must be the producer. A stout man with a crooked tie talked rapidly to the petite woman whom Mollie knew to be the casting director.

Mollie looked back down at the script and wondered if she'd be able to read it without stuttering. She couldn't remember being so nervous in her entire life. The part itself didn't look hard; Jill, the character in the script, seemed basically nice, if a bit given to mishaps. At one point, Jill had to stumble over a scatter rug; Mollie giggled, she could do that part without any problem!

"Is it funny?" someone asked.

Mollie raised her eyes quickly. She looked around and saw a young man in T-shirt and jeans, with shaggy hair and friendly brown eyes partly hidden by thick glasses. At first glance, he seemed to be in his late teens, but closer inspection revealed a more mature look about him that made Mollie guess he might be in his twenties. She relaxed.

"Yes," Mollie said. "I like this girl. She's a lot like me."

"Nice average teenager, you mean?" the young man asked.

Mollie frowned. There were many words she would have used to describe herself, depending on the mood she was in at the moment, but "average" would never be one of them.

"No," she told him. "She seems to get into trouble a lot. I understand that."

The young man grinned. "You get into scrapes, too?"

"It's not really my fault." Mollie's tone was earnest. "Things just seem to happen to me." She lowered her voice, glancing toward the table, and told him about the mishap with the margarine tubs that had brought her to the attention of Nicole's photographer. The young man laughed aloud.

Grinning herself, Mollie went on to tell him about the day she had almost burned down the house trying to scramble some eggs. She then detailed the spy thriller she and Cindy had concocted when they discovered Nicole going off to secret meetings that later turned out to be modeling classes.

"I see what you mean," the young man said. "I think you're wasted as an actress, Mollie. You should be writing the show."

Mollie grinned, but then looked to see that the group behind the table had at last stopped talking and was watching her expectantly. She flushed, afraid that by talking to a stagehand, she'd been holding up the audition.

"I think they're ready for you now," the young man said, as if in affirmation. Mollie gulped hard and stood up, approaching the table.

"And you are . . ." the woman looked down, rifling through her notes.

"Mollie Lewis." Her voice came out in a squeak, and Mollie swallowed hard again.

"All right, Mollie, turn to the middle of page three. Start with 'I've got a great idea.' "

Mollie read several pages as Jill, while one woman read for the other characters. Mollie glanced up once or twice, trying to gauge the reactions of the people at the table, but they seemed almost bored. There was certainly no sign of appreciation or amazement at having found exactly the right person for the part. Mollie's hopes began to dwindle. When she finished reading, she paused, watching as they scribbled a few notes on the pads in front of them, and asked, "Would you like me to fall over the rug? I'm quite good at that."

The woman who seemed to be the spokesperson for the group looked at Mollie blankly. Mollie heard a slight chuckle to the side of the room and knew that the young stagehand at least understood. But the woman shook her head and said matter-of-factly, "That's all for now, Mollie. If we need you to read again, we'll give you a call."

"Oh, okay," Molly said, feeling the whole thing had been anticlimactic. "Thank you."

The same young woman who had called her in motioned her toward the door, where Mrs. Lewis joined her daughter, giving her an unobtrusive pat on the shoulder.

As they left the building, Mrs. Lewis said, "That was a wonderful reading, Mollie. You did a terrific job."

"I was awful," Mollie sighed. "They didn't even smile when I read the funny parts."

"You did your best, Mollie," her mother reminded her gently. "Now we'll have to wait and see. There are a lot of girls trying out, you know."

"I know," Mollie said. "I shouldn't expect a miracle."

Yet it was hard not to hope. She and her mother found a coffee shop and had a quick sandwich, then started the drive home before rush hour traffic could clog the freeways. After her sleepless night, Mollie found the slight motion of the car extremely soothing. She felt her head nodding. When she woke, they were turning into their own driveway.

When they entered the kitchen, Cindy was sitting at the breakfast table with another Dagwood sandwich, and Nicole, hearing the door shut, hurried in from the hall.

"What happened?" both girls exclaimed, almost in unison. "How'd it go, Mollie?"

"I was awful," Mollie groaned, convinced that she hadn't impressed anyone.

"Not at all," Mrs. Lewis contradicted, taking off her coat. "Mollie gave a fine reading."

"Your opinion doesn't count. You're my mother," Mollie pointed out gloomily.

Mrs. Lewis ignored the interruption. "However, there were an awful lot of girls there trying out, so, who knows?"

"Cheer up, Mollie," Nicole said. "At least you got to try out."

Mollie, remembering her first abortive attempt to enter the world of films, brightened slightly.

"You probably weren't half as bad as you think," Cindy encouraged, between bites of her sandwich.

"Thanks, I think," Mollie murmured.

"Look," Nicole told her. "I stopped at the news

stand on the way home from school and bought a copy of *Variety*. There's a short paragraph about the sitcom pilot and a picture of the producer, Ty Brenner. He's supposed to be a real Hollywood boy wonder."

"I saw him," Mollie said. "Long face and a beard."

Nicole looked puzzled. "No." She handed the paper to Mollie. "No beard."

Mollie took the paper and studied the fuzzy photograph—the blurred newspaper photo left no doubt. It was the friendly young man in jeans whom Mollie had spoken to so frankly.

"Oh, no," Mollie cried. "It's *him*!"

They all stared at her in bewilderment.

"I thought he was a stagehand. I told him everything!"

"Everything?" Nicole raised her brows.

"About knocking over the table full of margarine, and—well, too much. He knows what a klutz I am!"

Mollie, sure that she had lost any chance of getting the part, had to blink back tears.

"Nice going, shrimp," Cindy murmured.

Mollie was too depressed to even glare at her sister. "I need something to eat," she moaned. "Any chocolate chip ice cream left?"

Nicole and Mrs. Lewis exchanged a glance just as the phone rang in the hall.

"I'll get it," Cindy yelled. "It's probably Grant. He said he would call."

She made a dash for the telephone, while Mollie, ready to ease her sorrow with a generous helping of ice cream, opened the freezer compartment, and peered inside.

She had just pulled out the container of ice cream when Cindy reappeared in the doorway, a curious expression on her face.

"Better put it back, shrimp. I hear that TV cameras add ten pounds to your appearance."

"What?"

"That was the studio. They want you to come back tomorrow for another reading."

Chapter 9

*M*ollie promptly dropped the ice cream on her toe when she heard Cindy's announcement. Hopping around the kitchen in mingled pain and joy, she yelled, "I don't believe it!"

Nicole hurried to rescue the ice cream before Winston could thrust his inquisitive muzzle into it. "That's great, Mollie," she exclaimed. "I'm so happy for you."

"I've got to call Sarah." Mollie stopped nursing her injured toe and headed for the stairs. "And Linda and Heather and Arlene."

"Mollie," Laura Lewis admonished, "better get started on your assignments. You still have school-work to do, remember."

"Oh, Mom," Mollie moaned. When she reached the second floor, she headed for the telephone.

Sarah was suitably impressed with Mollie's big news. "Boy, that's really exciting, Mollie," the other girl said. "I told you you'd be famous."

"I'm not there yet," Mollie reminded her cautiously. "But I've got past the first hurdle. That's something."

"I'm green with envy," her friend assured her. "Good luck tomorrow."

"I'll need it." Then Mollie remembered her mother's words. "I've got to start my makeup work. How was school today?"

"Same old stuff," Sarah answered. "In science, Mrs. Ratcliff did an experiment with magnets, and when she left the room, Howard used the magnets to pull down the zipper on Jane Ann's jumpsuit."

"Oh no," Mollie said with a giggle. "What'd she do?"

"Poured a bowl of algae over his head. He was a mess," Sarah said. "It was a riot."

Mollie felt vaguely left out and she said, "I wish I'd been there to see it."

"But you had a much more exciting day," Sarah reminded her. "Oh, Mollie, the drama club is planning a hay ride this Friday night. Who do you think you'll ask?"

"Probably David," Mollie said, remembering the cute sophomore she had met in art club. "That is, if I even get to go; Mom and Dad said I had to get all my schoolwork done before doing anything else."

"I hope you can go. It should be a lot of fun," Sarah said.

"Yes," Mollie agreed. "Talk to you later."

She made a few more quick calls, then hung up the phone and went into her room, dropping onto her bed with a sigh. Opening her algebra book, Mollie looked at the symbols as if she'd never seen them before. She was too tired to think, but if she didn't get all this work done, she'd have to work all weekend. She picked up a pencil and tried to concentrate.

Mollie and her mother made another early start the next morning, and this time when they arrived at the studio building, they found a much smaller group of girls assembled in the waiting room. Mrs. Lewis took a seat beside one of the other mothers. Mollie, feeling those familiar pangs of nervousness, brightened when she recognized Roberta sitting at one end of the room.

"Hi." Mollie walked over and sat down beside the other girl, who smiled in greeting.

"You made the first cut, too."

"I couldn't believe it," Mollie confessed. "They didn't look very impressed when I read yesterday."

"It's always like that," Roberta told her. "You just never know."

"What happens today?" Mollie asked, knowing that the other girl had had more experience with auditions.

"More readings, and a lot of waiting around," Roberta said, sounding resigned.

"Oh." Mollie, noting the history textbook Roberta was holding, wished that she had thought to bring some of her own work. The other girl went back to her book, and Mollie, spying a stack of magazines on a table across the room, walked over to find something to read. She selected a battered magazine and stood there leafing through it, when she heard a door open.

Glancing up, Mollie was stunned to discover herself not three feet from a young man whose jet black hair, dark eyes, and wicked smile were familiar from frequent viewing of his latest video on MTV.

"Ricky Thorne!" Mollie gasped, as the magazine slipped from her fingers.

The young rock star paused and bent to retrieve the periodical. "You dropped your magazine," he said pleasantly.

Unable to speak, Mollie smiled weakly and accepted the magazine, only able to mutter a hoarse "Thank you" after he had already walked away.

"Ricky Thorne!" Mollie couldn't believe this stroke of good luck. She walked back and sat down beside Roberta. "Did you see him?" she whispered.

The other girl also looked a bit awed. "Don't you know?" she said. "He has the lead in this sitcom pilot. We're auditioning to play his younger sister."

Acting on the same set with Ricky Thorne! Mollie thought she might faint. "Pinch me," she murmured. "I must be in heaven."

Roberta giggled and went back to her textbook.

Cindy came home from school, dropped her books on the kitchen counter, and gave Winston a pat. "Anybody else home, boy?"

He pushed his big shaggy head against her legs, and Cindy obligingly patted him again.

"I guess not." She answered her own question. "Nicole stayed at school for a yearbook meeting, and Mom's car isn't here, so I guess she and Mollie are still in the big city getting famous."

Winston watched her gravely.

"Not that I don't want her to get the part, old boy," Cindy assured the big dog, going to the refrigerator to look for a snack as he followed eagerly behind her. "It's just that with Nicole and her modeling, and now Mollie becoming a hot shot actress—I feel like the dud of the family, you know?"

Winston wagged his tail eagerly, although Cindy suspected that he was more interested in the lunch meat she had taken from the fridge than in her question.

She made herself a sandwich, slipped Winston a piece of ham, and sat down at the table. A couple of books on the counter caught her eye, and she picked up one to read as she ate her snack. "One of Mollie's books on show business," she told Winston. "Who would want to be an actress, anyhow, and wear tons of makeup and spend all that time changing clothes? Yuck."

She flipped through the pages of the book until a picture attracted her attention. "Say, look at this," Cindy murmured to herself. "Now *this* is more like it!"

She was still absorbed in the book when the phone rang. Cindy reached for the phone and answered absently.

Grant's familiar voice said, "Hi, Cindy. Want to go to Taco Rio for a Coke?"

"There's something else I want to do," Cindy told him. "Meet me at the vacant lot at the end of our street in ten minutes."

"Okay." Grant sounded puzzled, but Cindy was in too much of a hurry to enlighten him now. She cleared away the crumbs from her snack and ran to get her bike out of the garage. Winston followed hopefully behind her.

"Want a run, Winnie?" Cindy asked him. "You can come." She located some odds and ends in the garage, then jumped on her bike, and set off, the big dog loping alongside.

When she reached the open stretch of land at the end of the street, Cindy stopped to let Winston catch up and soon saw Grant's broad-shouldered form in his red Trans Am come into view.

"Hi!" she waved, and in a moment he pulled up alongside her.

"What's going on, Cindy?"

"I've got this *terrific* idea. I looked through one of Mollie's show business books, and—"

Grant snorted in derision. "Don't tell me you've decided to become an actress, too?"

"Of course not." Cindy's answer was indignant. "I've got more sense than that. But I found this neat chapter all about doing stunts. Talk about interesting work!"

"Cindy, you've got to be kidding." Grant frowned. "That type of thing is dangerous, even for people with experience. You don't know what you're doing—you'd break your neck."

Only slightly daunted by Grant's discouraging

reaction, Cindy threw him an impatient glance. "I'll start with something *easy*. I'm not nuts."

"I'm not so sure about that," Grant muttered. But he was familiar with Cindy's stubborn streak, and though his brow wrinkled in anxiety as he listened to her talk, Grant finally decided that if Cindy was determined to try this, he'd better go along to pick up the pieces.

"What are you going to do?"

"I used to do great wheelies when I was a kid," Cindy told him. "Let's take this old barrel down to the beach, and I'll try some jumps. The sand will be soft if I fall."

Grant still looked skeptical, but he helped her pull the rusty old barrel down toward the beach, quite deserted under the pale February sun. Winston followed them patiently for a while, but finally lost interest and headed off down the beach.

When Cindy had the barrel positioned to her satisfaction, she retrieved her bike and took up her position twenty feet away.

"Here I go!"

She pedaled furiously to get up speed and tried to lift the bike at just the right moment—only to ram squarely into the barrel. The hollow metal cylinder echoed with the impact, and Cindy flew over the handlebars, hitting the barrel, then sliding unceremoniously into the sand.

"Are you all right?" Grant yelled, running up to examine her.

Cindy looked dazed, but in one piece.

"Sure," she grinned. "Nothing to it. Except I need to get up more speed, I think."

She picked up her bike, dusted the sand off her jeans, and took up her stance again, this time further down the beach. But this run also ended in disaster.

Cindy, groaning this time as she rubbed a bruised elbow, sat up looking perplexed. "I need something to lift me up for take off," she decided. "Look for a piece of wood."

They went back to the vacant lot and searched through the abandoned rubble that littered one end. Cindy grinned as she pulled out a broad piece of plywood that had been half buried in the sand. "This should do it."

With Grant's reluctant help, Cindy propped the board up with several pieces of driftwood and a couple of cement blocks from the vacant lot, then wheeled her bike back to the starting point.

"This time I'm going to make it," she called.

Grant shut his eyes and crossed his fingers on both hands.

Cindy pedaled hard and picked up more speed than before. She approached the plywood platform, feeling the cold wind rushing against her face, grinning in exultation. This time she'd do it!

As the bike hit the improvised platform, the plywood, weakened by exposure and age, cracked loudly, and instead of propelling her upward, Cindy and her bike took an abrupt nose dive toward the barrel, hitting the metal can hard.

Cindy went flying over the handlebars once again, and hit the sand head first.

Grant ran to her, an alarmed expression on his face. "Cindy! Are you hurt? Is anything broken?"

This time it took her a moment to catch her breath. The beach whirled around her at an alarming rate. For a moment it seemed that *everything* hurt. Then Cindy sat up slowly as her dizziness receded. Her elbow was grazed, and her shin scraped, both stung; and . . .

"There's blood on your face!" Grant gazed at her in distress.

"It's okay, it's just a scratch." Cindy felt her forehead gingerly, wincing as she touched the scraped skin.

"Here." Grant handed her a handkerchief, and she wiped her face. Beneath the scratches, she looked pale, and Grant's concern increased.

"I think you should see a doctor."

"For a few scratches?" Cindy tried to laugh, but the sound that emerged was weak. "Of course not." She touched the back of her head, but didn't mention that she could feel a sizable bump forming. Remembering her boating accident back in the fall, Cindy wondered if she could be suffering from another concussion. Probably not, she decided optimistically. She was beginning to feel more like herself, already.

"I'm okay, really," she tried to assure Grant, touched by his concern.

"Maybe," he said, his voice dry. "But your bike's not so lucky."

"Oh no!" Upset for the first time, Cindy stood up carefully, going closer to inspect her battered cycle. The front wheel was twisted at an odd angle, and there was major damage to the rest of the bike.

She whistled under her breath, wondering what her parents would say. She might be able to hide *her* scratches and bruises, but the wrecked bicycle would be impossible to disguise.

"Are you ready to go home?" Grant asked.

"Well, I guess so," Cindy admitted. She couldn't do any more stunts without her bicycle, anyway.

"Let's go to your house and work on your injuries," Grant said. "Maybe we can even fix up your bike some."

Cindy made a face at him, but was glad to have his help as they cleared the junk off the beach, collected her damaged bike, and headed for home.

When Mollie and Mrs. Lewis reached home at last, darkness had fallen, and the lights inside the Spanish-style ranch house gave it a warm, hospitable look. Laura Lewis parked the station wagon in the garage, then stretched her cramped muscles and climbed out of the car.

"This commuting to Los Angeles gets tiring very quickly," she said.

Mollie, who had been dozing again, looked guilty. But nothing could diminish her high spirits for very long. She skipped across the garage and followed her mother inside the kitchen, where they were greeted by a savory, meaty aroma.

"Something smells good," Mrs. Lewis said, smiling. "Thank you, Nicole. I certainly wasn't looking forward to cooking dinner after that drive."

"It wasn't me," Nicole said. "I stayed late after school for a yearbook meeting. Cindy made tacos. We saved you some."

"My goodness." Mrs. Lewis looked a bit startled. Cooking wasn't one of Cindy's favorite occupations. "Then it's you I should thank, Cindy. This was very thoughtful of you."

Cindy, her back to them as she opened the microwave oven door to take out the crisp shells and meat filling, felt a twinge of guilt. The decision to cook dinner had not been a completely altruistic one. She figured that she'd better explain how she had managed to wreck her bike.

"I didn't mind," she murmured now, feeling a bit dishonest for accepting her mother's praise. She set the tacos on the table and turned to get the bowls of shredded lettuce, tomatoes, peppers and cheese.

"Cindy!" Mrs. Lewis's tone sharpened. "What on earth did you do to your face?"

"It's nothing." Cindy touched the scratches and bruises and tried to sound offhand. "Just took a spill on my bike. No big deal."

Her mother sighed. "Come into the bathroom and let me take a look. Did you wash the dirt out of the scratches?"

"Yes," Cindy said. "Your tacos are going to get cold."

Her mother gave her a stern look, and Cindy shrugged and followed her into the bathroom.

"How did it go today?" Nicole asked her youngest sister. "You look like you're on Cloud Nine."

"I am, Nicole," Mollie breathed, hugging herself and dancing around the kitchen. "They already told me to come back Friday. Tomorrow Mom has to take me to apply for a theatrical work permit. I think I'm really going to make it!"

Nicole's eyes widened. "You got the part?"

"Well, not yet," Mollie confessed. "But I'm still being considered. And that means a lot, Nicole."

"Don't get overconfident, Mollie." Nicole looked at her little sister with some concern. It was just like Mollie to jump to conclusions—justified or not—making her disappointment even more bitter if she didn't get the role.

"I won't," Mollie answered, refusing to allow her blissful state to be marred by harsh reality. "But let me tell you the rest. You'll never guess in a *million* years who's going to star in the sitcom!"

"Judging from your expression, it must be good." Nicole's tone was dry.

"Guess!"

"Paul Newman."

"No, silly. Even better." Mollie couldn't withhold her secret any longer. "Ricky Thorne!"

"Ricky Thorne—the singer?" Nicole raised her eyebrows, impressed despite herself. "*Vraiment?*"

"Honest! I saw him today at the studio. And Nicole—he *spoke* to me! I think he likes me!"

"Oh no," Nicole murmured.

Cindy and Mrs. Lewis came back into the kitchen, and Nicole began to set places for the latecomers. "How many tacos do you want, Mollie?"

"Just one."

Cindy looked at her sister in surprise. "Are you sick?"

"Worse," Nicole told her. "In love!"

Chapter 10

*W*hen the buzzing of her alarm finally penetrated Mollie's consciousness Friday morning, she groaned and ducked under the covers, trying to escape the unwelcome summons. But it was no use. Yawning, Mollie reached out to click off the buzzer and managed to push herself out of bed. Five o'clock. This was ridiculous, she told herself grumpily. She had studied her script until late last night, and she felt as if she'd just gotten into bed.

The thought of seeing Ricky Thorne again lifted her spirits slightly, but even that reminder couldn't keep her drooping eyelids from trying to close again. With great effort, she stumbled into the bathroom.

By the time Mollie had pulled on some clothes and dragged herself downstairs, her father was already at the breakfast table sipping a cup of hot coffee.

"Dad," Mollie exclaimed in surprise. "What are you doing up so early?"

"Your mother and I talked it over last night. She's exhausted from driving to Los Angeles every day, and she's way behind at the shop. We decided that since I didn't have anything pressing, I would accompany you today."

Mollie flushed, feeling a rush of guilt. Even though her mother had an assistant at her catering shop, Laura Lewis still played an important role in keeping everything on schedule. The thought of her mother's business suffering—because of her—made Mollie wince.

Richard Lewis, correctly interpreting Mollie's expression, pointed out gently, "We agreed that you would have your chance, Mollie, since it means so much to you. But it hasn't been easy on your mother."

"I know," Mollie said. "I really appreciate it, honest."

"I'm sure you do," her dad said. "But it wouldn't hurt to remind your mother now and then."

He looked at his watch and took one last sip of coffee. "We'd better go. Rush hour is already upon us."

Mollie followed him out to the big sedan, remembering to collect a stack of schoolwork to add to her script and the change of clothes in her tote bag.

When they reached the studio after the long drive, Mollie added her name to the sign-in sheet. She was awed to discover that only three other girls had been called back this time. Roberta was there, and two girls that Mollie had spoken to only briefly.

While her dad took a seat in the back of the room, Mollie went up to speak to Roberta.

"Glad to see you're still here," she told the other girl. And the funny thing was that it was true, despite the fact that Mollie was beginning to suspect that Roberta might be her strongest competition. A friendly face was always nice to see.

"What do we do today, have you heard?"

Roberta looked up from her book and Mollie thought the girl looked tense. "We're doing test shots with Ricky."

"Gosh." Mollie gulped hard. How would she ever remember the lines she had memorized last night with *Ricky Thorne* on the same set? "Would you like to practice with me while we wait to be called?" she asked.

Roberta shook her head. "No, thanks."

Mollie, feeling rebuffed, tried to sound casual. "Well, talk to you later, then."

So much for the friendly face! Was Roberta being standoffish because she was afraid Mollie might take the part away from her? Mollie remembered all the tales she had heard about Hollywood cutthroat competition. Still, she had not expected it from another teenager. Sighing, she went back to sit beside her father and tried to study her lines.

When Mollie was convinced that she knew the part backward and forward, she tried to do some schoolwork, but found she couldn't concentrate on algebra equations while she waited to be called to the set. When they finally called her to makeup, Mollie went eagerly.

A young man gave her hair a few skillful strokes that made her look much more stylish, and sprayed it until she thought she couldn't breathe. Then he sent Mollie on to the next room.

Draped in a white cloth, she sat in a big chair watching the makeup technician's expert handling of all the tubes and jars. Her skill awed Mollie almost as much as meeting a famous star.

"What an interesting job you have," Mollie told the young woman sincerely. Mollie, who loved to experiment with different kinds of makeup, thought that doing faces all day must be great fun.

The young brunette grinned at Mollie. "It's hard on the feet, but I like it. I feel like an artist with a blank canvas. I look at each face and try to see just what I can do to achieve the best results."

Mollie watched in the big mirror as the young woman's hands moved deftly across her face. She noticed that her blue eyes were subtly enhanced, her lips gleamed with color, and her cheeks now held a healthy glow.

"Wow," she said. "I look great."

The makeup technician laughed quietly at Mollie's appreciation of her talents. "Glad you like it," she told her. "Are you going to wardrobe today?"

Mollie shook her head in regret. "They told us to wear our own clothes, and nothing fancy." Mollie, who would have loved the excuse to buy a new dress, sighed, her disappointment obvious.

The young woman gave her a sympathetic grin. "Maybe next time. My roommate works in the wardrobe department. When you get to be a star, they keep a wardrobe dummy scaled to your exact proportions. Sometimes we go through the storage room and try to guess who the stars are by the shapes of their dummies."

Mollie giggled at the thought. Then one of the assistant directors called her name, and she stood up quickly, while the makeup technician pulled off the cloth and dusted the excess powder from her face.

"Thanks," Mollie said. "You did a great job with my face."

"You're welcome," the woman said. "Good luck."

Mollie followed the assistant director back to the main set, her stomach beginning to tighten as her big moment approached. She saw her father sitting in the background, reading a newspaper. He looked up to give her an encouraging smile. Mollie's answering grin felt a bit wobbly.

Standing at the back of the set, she could see how the other side of the living room would look so convincing to the cameras. From where Mollie stood, she could see that the room was only a shell—its walls propped up by slanting supports, with the front of the room open for the big wheeled cameras. Hanging from the high ceiling of the studio were dozens of oversize lights, and the glare of the big bulbs made the temperature in the room seem warmer than a desert. Mollie could feel beads of perspiration forming on her forehead already—though whether from the heat under the lamps or nervousness, or both—she couldn't say.

The director, Jake—the man with the beard who had sat in on the first auditions—motioned Mollie forward.

"This is your mark, Mollie." He pointed to a chalk mark on the floor as Mollie stared down at her feet. "I want you to walk through the doorway, come to this mark, and start your lines, okay?"

Mollie nodded.

"Let's run through it."

Mollie walked to the side of the set, turned, and prepared to make her entrance.

"*Now*, Mollie."

She opened the door and walked forward, trying to stop at the right place without actually looking down at the floor. "Where's the party, people?" she asked brightly, glad that she had devoted so much time to learning her lines.

"Good," the director said. "Go back and take your place again, Mollie. Rick!"

Mollie returned to the side of the set. In answer to the director's summons, the young rock star walked in from the other side and took his position on the set.

"Cameras ready," the director commanded. "Now, Mollie."

Mollie opened the set door once more, paused for one heart-stopping moment at the sight of Ricky Thorne waiting on center stage, then forced her legs to carry her forward—straight into a side table, sending the brass lamp on its polished surface plummeting to the floor.

Mollie, making a futile grab for the lamp, thought she might faint. "I'm sorry," she gasped.

"It's okay," the director told her. "These things happen. Go back and try it again."

One of the assistants straightened the lamp and the table. Mollie, sorry that she had ever dreamed of being an actress, retreated to the sidelines, wishing that she could delay long enough for the red in her cheeks to fade. But the director cued her once more, and she stalked forward, determined to walk in a straight line this time.

She made it to the center of the set without walking into any of the furniture, only to have the director call, "You're off your mark, Mollie."

Even more flustered, Mollie retreated to try it again. She stared at the chalk mark—engraving its location on her brain—afraid to even *look* at Ricky Thorne, who waited patiently for her to get it right. She started again. She made it to the correct position, looked at Ricky—whose answering grin made her heart beat more quickly—and spoke her line loudly.

"Where's the people, party?"

Mollie put both hands to her face. Ricky chuckled and someone behind the cameras groaned.

"I'm sorry," she gasped.

"It's okay, sweetheart," the rock star told her. "It happens to the best of us, honest. I flub my lines all the time. Just relax."

Mollie flashed him a grateful smile and prepared to begin again. The sight of those dark eyes focused upon her made her almost forget her chagrin. And he had called her "sweetheart"! Wait till she told her friends. Feeling much better, she started over.

It took the rest of the morning before the director was satisfied with their one short scene. Mollie, wondering privately just how long it took to shoot a thirty-minute show, was relieved to hear the director announce a lunch break. She felt hollow to the core.

As the set cleared, Mollie glanced hopefully toward Ricky, hoping that he might ask her to have lunch with him. Instead, the young star began a conversation with the director, and they walked off the set together.

Mollie sighed, but consoled herself with the thought that it was business, after all, that took him away. At least Ricky hadn't gone off with any of the other young actresses. Mollie still harbored the delightful conviction that Ricky's obvious preference for her was becoming even more marked. Look at how nice he had been during the taping.

She found her father waiting at the back of the set. "Shall we try out the studio cafeteria?" Mr. Lewis asked.

Mollie nodded. "I'm starved!"

When they joined the foodline, Mollie had to restrain herself from buying everything she saw, reminding herself that television actresses had to watch their weight with an eagle eye. She settled for cottage cheese with fruit and a glass of milk. Richard Lewis, watching his daughter's unusual self-discipline with a smile, took a club sandwich with potato salad.

They sat down at a small table, and Mollie

nodded to the other two girls from the set. "Where's Roberta?" she asked them.

"She's eating in the dressing room," one of the girls answered.

Mollie, wondering why Roberta seemed to be avoiding them, shook her head. She finished her scanty lunch quickly—and sneaked a bit of her father's potato salad.

"Is acting worth giving up food, Mollie?" her dad asked.

"Sure," Mollie said, trying to sound convinced. She glanced over at the array of desserts, then turned her eyes away.

When they returned to the set, Mollie found a young woman with short hair and a firm gaze awaiting them.

"This is Ms. Carey, your studio teacher," the assistant director told the girls.

Mollie made a face, and Roberta, who had rejoined the group, murmured, "Didn't you know we have to have three hours of schooling on the set every day?"

"No," Mollie grumbled. "How dreadful."

They all followed the teacher to the room set aside for them. Mollie, with a sigh, took out the schoolwork she had brought along. This was *not* how she had pictured the life of a rising young star.

By the time they left the studio and fought their way home through the rush-hour traffic, the sun had long since set. Mollie walked into the Lewis home, her shoulders drooping with weariness.

"How are you, Mollie?" her mother asked, a

note of concern in her voice. "I've got some roast beef and Yorkshire pudding for you—although the pudding has collapsed, I'm afraid. And you're supposed to call Sarah."

"I will," Mollie said. "In just a minute."

She climbed the stairs slowly, dropped her tote bag in the middle of the floor, and eyed her bed wistfully. She had to call Sarah, wash her hands, and go back downstairs to eat. All Mollie really wanted to do was lie down across her comfortable bed. "Just for a minute," she promised herself, falling onto the rumpled covers. The bed felt heavenly. Despite her resolve, Mollie's eyes drifted shut.

When she opened them again, she couldn't remember for a moment where she was. "Time to get up?" she murmured to herself. Then she realized that the soft rumbling in her ear was not the sound of her alarm. It was Cinders, curled up against her in a contented knot, purring loudly.

"My gosh, what time is it?" Mollie sat up abruptly, to the cat's annoyance. He stopped purring and regarded her sternly.

"The hayride!" Mollie wailed, staring at her clock. "I've missed it!"

She ran downstairs to find the kitchen empty. Her parents were sitting quietly in the den. "Why didn't you wake me?" she demanded.

Mrs. Lewis looked up in surprise. "You looked so tired, Mollie, I thought dinner could wait."

"Who cares about dinner?" Mollie wailed. "I've slept through half of the drama club hayride. It's too late to go, now!"

Her parents exchanged glances. "Mollie," Mrs. Lewis told her gently, "we told you when you began the auditions that you'd have to give up some things. There are only so many hours in the day. You do have to eat and sleep *and* get your schoolwork done before you can go out with your friends. You simply have to be aware that some sacrifices are required."

Mollie—remembering that she wasn't the only one who had made sacrifices this week—bit back her angry retort and sighed instead.

Chapter 11

As Nicole walked softly down the stairs early Saturday morning, she glanced through the doorway of Mollie's room and saw Mollie still buried beneath the bedcovers. The poor kid's exhausted, Nicole thought. At least she can sleep late today.

Which, unfortunately, was more than Nicole could do. She had gotten up early for her modeling session downtown. Though she knew that her hair would be redone at the studio, Nicole had taken a few minutes herself to try for a more glamorous effect. She still nursed a slight feeling of inadequacy, remembering that the photographer had thought her favorite hairstyle boring.

Using a lot of styling gel, and inspired by a picture she had seen in a fashion magazine, Nicole finally achieved a look that she decided would be unusual enough to satisfy even the most jaded fashion expert. But when she glanced at herself in the hall mirror, her reflection was that of a stranger. Nicole, feeling like an imposter, sighed and went into the kitchen.

Cindy, dressed in a sweatsuit, leaned against the counter sipping a small glass of juice. She was up even earlier than usual for her Saturday run.

"What are you doing up at this hour?" Nicole demanded.

"It's nearly seven," Cindy answered. "I'm always up by now. What happened to you?" she demanded. "Did you get an electric shock from your curling iron?"

"No, silly." Nicole reached for the coffee maker. "I did this on purpose."

"Why?" Cindy continued to stare.

"One of the photographers didn't like my hair the other day. I thought I should try something more unusual."

"You look unusual, all right. You look like you came straight out of a midnight horror show." Cindy continued to watch her sister, looking puzzled. "I think you're letting this modeling business go to your head, Nicole."

Nicole flushed. "I just want to look in style, that's all."

Cindy shook her head. "This whole family is going crazy. First Mollie, now you."

Nicole, anxious to change the topic of conversation, pushed the button on the coffee maker and asked, "Where's Dad? Isn't he jogging with you this morning?"

Cindy shook her head. "He had to go down to

the office to catch up on some work that he couldn't do yesterday because he went to L.A. with Mollie. Do you think the shrimp realizes how much trouble she's putting the whole family through?"

"Probably not," Nicole said. "Mollie can be pretty single-minded, you know that. And she wants this role awfully bad." Nicole poured herself a cup of coffee. "What did Dad say about you wrecking your bike?"

Cindy grimaced at the memory of her dad's scolding. "You don't want to know," she told her sister. "Got to run." She tied her shoes in double knots and set out at a fast lope.

Nicole took a sip of the steaming coffee, then looked at the clock on the wall. "*Mon dieu*, so do I."

After Cindy completed her morning run, she came home and consumed a mammoth bowl of cereal with a couple of bananas to top it off. Then she showered, pulled on clean jeans and a sweater, and went downstairs to wait for Grant.

When the red Trans Am pulled into the drive, Cindy ran out and pulled open the door, dropping into the passenger's seat. "Gorgeous day, isn't it?"

Grant, glancing at the gray clouds that hung low over the California coastline, grinned slightly. "If you say so. Where to?"

"Let's drive down to the beach."

Grant nodded, but he examined Cindy's expression with a wary eye. She was up to something.

Sure enough. Cindy continued, eyeing him hopefully, "Feel like giving me a driving lesson today?"

"No," Grant answered firmly. He turned off the ignition, and the low hum of the car's engine died.

Cindy frowned at him. "Why not?"

"Not while you've got stunt-fever!"

"I wouldn't do anything to your car," Cindy protested, trying to look as if the thought of stunt driving hadn't been lurking in the back of her mind.

"You wouldn't *mean* to," Grant corrected. "But you're in a funny mood this week, Cindy."

"No, I'm not."

"You're usually pretty smart, but lately—I don't know. When we go horseback riding tomorrow, you'll probably try doing somersaults from the saddle. What's going on, anyhow?"

Just why his question struck a spark wasn't clear to her, but Cindy's temper flared. "Nothing!" she snapped.

"So why this sudden interest in performing stunts?"

"I thought it sounded interesting, that's all," Cindy replied hotly.

"I think you've flipped out. You've got more guts than any kid I know, but usually you have some sense, too. These stunts of yours are plain crazy. Stuntmen are trained professionals, with special props and extra safeguards, and they still get hurt a lot—sometimes even killed!"

"If you think I can't do it just because I'm a girl—" Cindy began.

Grant's blue eyes turned cold. "You know better than that. I thought that stupid surfing contest was the last time we'd get hung up on this battle of the sexes thing. You've gone off the deep end, Cindy."

Cindy flushed angrily, hearing in his statement an echo of her own words to Nicole. "Thanks for the instant analysis, doctor!"

"I'm beginning to think you're jealous of your sisters—Nicole with her modeling, and Mollie trying to become a TV star."

"I am not!" Cindy, stung by this unexpected accusation, glared at the tall boy. She pushed open the car door and jumped out. "If you think you can tell me what to do, Grant MacPhearson—"

He met her angry gaze squarely. "Trying hard to be the best surfer or the best swimmer might stretch your physical abilities to the limit, but at least there's a good reason. This is just stupid. I care too much about you to stand and watch you risk your neck for nothing."

"Then don't watch!" Cindy yelled and stalked back up the driveway. So much for her day with Grant! Of all the conceited, overbearing pompous, bossy—her stock of adjectives momentarily depleted, Cindy gritted her teeth. When Grant had turned a corner and was safely out of sight, Cindy, feeling suddenly aimless, walked back into the garage. She found Winston, lying with his head on his paws, watching her patiently.

"Didn't try to follow me today, did you, old boy?" Cindy murmured, petting the big dog. "Didn't want to get in the middle of that ugly scene."

Now that her anger had cooled slightly, Cindy sat down on the back steps beside the dog and wished she could take back her impulsive remarks to Grant. "Same old Lewis—big mouth and all," she muttered.

An awful thought occurred to her. Was Grant right? Was she simply jealous of all the extra attention Mollie and Nicole had received because of their new occupations?

"Maybe just a little," she confessed to Winston. "But why can't I try something new, too? I won't do any more stupid stunts," she told the dog. "This time I'll stick to something simple."

So what kind of possibilities did that leave? The ocean was too rough today to surf, even with a wetsuit to protect her from the cold. Nobody did stunts in softball, or none that Cindy could think of.

"There must be something I can do, Winnie," she told the dog, who lifted his ears slightly. She wandered back into the kitchen and picked up the morning paper from the breakfast table. Glancing through the folded pages, Cindy found the entertainment section and scanned the movie ads. An ad for a new martial arts movie caught her eye.

"Hey, that would be fun, I bet," Cindy murmured. She grinned at Winston. "Time for some research, boy."

Whistling, she picked up Mollie's overdue library books, checked her pockets for change, and headed for the bus stop. An hour later she was home again with several books on martial arts, some with marvelous illustrations and diagrams.

"This is more like it," Cindy told the dog, as he listened patiently. She skimmed through the volumes, sure that she could master this new skill without any problem.

"Martial arts movies are always popular," she told Winston. "If I can do this, I could get lots of stunt work."

With Grant's accusation still lingering in her mind, Cindy promised herself that she'd do nothing extreme. First she stretched, warming up as the books suggested so she didn't pull a muscle when she jumped and kicked.

"This is fun, Winnie," she murmured, pausing to push the big dog gently aside to make more room as she attempted a spinning back kick.

After a half-hour's hard workout, Cindy, the eternal optimist, began to feel more ambitious.

"There are some short pieces of wood in Dad's workbench," she told the dog. "Wonder if I could break one with a blow of my hand?"

Winston looked dubious.

"It can't be *that* hard to do," Cindy argued cheerfully. She headed for the workbench.

When Nicole reached the studio, she found the other models already assembled. She quickly doffed her street clothes and hurried to sit down before the hairstylist.

"Make sure you give me the latest style," she told him.

"Right."

Later, after Nicole's makeup had been completed, she pulled on a silver striped jumpsuit.

"You look like you just got off the last flying saucer from Mars," Judy, one of the other models, said.

"Don't I know it," Nicole agreed. "What do you think of my hair—no, don't answer that. What do you suppose the photographer will think?"

Judy looked her over critically. "Pretty far-out. He'll probably love it."

"I hope so." Nicole sighed. One of the assistants knocked on the dressing room door, and the girls hurried out to take their places in front of the cameras.

The shooting today seemed especially long and tedious. Nicole, craning her neck painfully at the photographer's instruction, remembered that a local art gallery had planned a special exhibit for this weekend. If this shoot didn't last all day, she'd love to go over there for a few hours.

"Hey, Nicky, move to your left and give me a dreamy look."

Nicole shifted her position and tried to unfocus her eyes. "I'm sick of people who never remember my real name," she murmured under her breath to Judy, who stifled a giggle.

"I know," the other model whispered. "They think of us as a collection of body parts!"

"Don't move your mouth!" the frustrated photographer pleaded—as if in confirmation—and the girls fell silent.

Nicole thought of the art gallery, and all the paintings she hadn't yet seen, the concerts she wanted to attend—the whole world of art and music and history that she loved so much—still waiting to be explored. College was the place to examine all those avenues.

Nicole suddenly knew that she couldn't pass up all those exciting possibilities just to be on the cover of a fashion magazine. Modeling part-time to make money for school was one thing, but Nicole was going to be more than a collection of hands and hair and lips.

Relieved to have come to a decision, Nicole stood up straighter.

"Nicky," the man behind the camera yelled. "You're blocking the girl behind you! Lean to your left."

Nicole leaned and, focusing her attention on the job at hand, smiled into the camera.

When Nicole reached home, the house seemed very quiet. She found a note from her mother on the refrigerator: "Gone to the catering shop, back at three."

Nicole took one last amused look at herself in the hall mirror and headed for the shower to wash away the stranger with the outer space hairdo. Reaching the top of the stairs, she noticed Mollie's bedroom door was shut. "Surely Mollie's not still sleeping," she said out loud.

"Don't bet on it," came the answer from the bathroom.

Nicole looked past the open door and gasped. "Cindy! What did you do to your hand?"

Cindy was soaking her hand and wrist in a

basin of ice cubes. She tried to smile, but the spreading bruise on the side of her hand was impossible to ignore.

"I've been reading some martial arts books from the library. I tried to break a block of wood, Bruce Lee–style."

"Cindy, you idiot! You can't learn karate from a book!"

"I found that out the hard way." Cindy managed a lopsided grin.

Nicole came closer and touched her sister's swollen hand gingerly. "Does it hurt?"

Cindy nodded. "The worst thing is, I'm supposed to go horseback riding with Grant tomorrow, and I think I've sprained my wrist. He'll kill me! Think I can ride a horse with one hand?"

Nicole shrugged. "You'll find a way if anyone can. But if you think Grant will be upset, wait till Mom finds out!"

Cindy groaned. "Let's face one disaster at a time." She wrapped her swollen hand in a towel and headed for the phone.

"What are you doing?"

"Calling Grant to tell him that my career as a stuntwoman just came to an abrupt end."

Chapter 12

$\mathcal{M}$ollie slept till well past noon, then crawled out of bed and took a long, luxurious soak in the tub. She finally dried off when she began to resemble a prune, then wrapped herself in a thick robe and wandered downstairs. She ate a huge breakfast, in defiance of weight-inducing cameras, and then, wondering where everyone was, went in search of her family.

She found Nicole sitting cross-legged on her bed, humming happily to herself as she pored over several college catalogues.

"What are you in such a good mood about?" Mollie demanded. "Meet a new guy?"

Nicole gave her little sister a condescending glance. "You wouldn't understand, Mol."

Mollie bristled. "Excuse me for living! Where is everybody?"

"Mom and Dad are both at work, and Cindy's

gone out with Grant. How did the test shots go yesterday?"

Mollie forgot her annoyance. "Pretty good, I think. Oh, Nicole, Ricky Thorne was so terrific! He helped me with the timing of my lines, and kept me on the right mark. I really think he likes me."

Nicole wrinkled her brow. "How old is he, Mollie?"

"I'm not sure," Mollie confessed. "Not that old, Nicole."

"I'd say in his early twenties, at least," Nicole speculated. "Too old for you, Mollie."

"I don't believe it," Mollie argued, her face flushing with anger. "The gossip column in *Teen Beat* said he just turned eighteen."

Nicole's tone was dry, but a glance at Mollie's obstinate expression made her shrug. "Have it your way, Mollie. But don't make something out of nothing."

"I'm not," Mollie protested. "He acts like I'm really special, Nicole. You weren't there."

"Whatever you say, Mol." Nicole had already returned to her college catalogues. Mollie stalked out of the bedroom, heading for the upstairs phone.

She dialed Sarah and found her eager to hear about the latest happenings in TV-land.

"Ricky was so great." Mollie repeated all the details for her friend's benefit. "He called me 'sweetheart'! I really think he likes me, Sarah."

"Gosh." Her friend sounded suitably awed. "You and Ricky will be an item in the Hollywood columns soon, Mollie. You must be so thrilled!"

"I am," Mollie agreed, then, remembering her uneventful evening the night before, added, "But I wish I could have gone to the hayride. How was it?"

"Oh, Mollie," Sarah said. "We had the best time! We rode out to the Thompsons' ranch, and all the stars were out. Everybody huddled under blankets and sang songs. Then we built a big bonfire and roasted hot dogs and marshmallows. It was so much fun."

"I wish I'd been there." Mollie felt a pang of regret. "I've never been on a hayride."

"The drama club will probably have another one next year," Sarah told her. "Since this one was such a success."

"Oh, that's good," Mollie said. But next year was an eternity away. "Did David go?"

There was a short pause on the other end of the line. Then her friend answered slowly, "Well, since you've got a big star interested in you, I guess you won't mind. David went with Sally Anderson."

"What?" Mollie sat up straighter, and discovered that she did mind, a lot. "That rat!"

"But, Mollie," Sarah reminded her, "the whole school knows about you and Ricky Thorne. How can you blame David for going out with someone else? You two weren't really going out, anyway."

"You're right, Sarah. I guess I can't," Mollie murmured. "Did he look like he had a good time?"

"I'm sure he'd rather have been with you," Sarah said loyally. "But Sally certainly had a wonderful time. She called Linda this morning and boasted that David will probably ask her to the Valentine's Dance."

"What?"

"It's only a couple of weeks away, and if you're still busy with the TV show . . ."

"I know," Mollie repeated, but she felt a keen sense of loss. All her friends would be having fun, and Mollie wouldn't be there.

"A bunch of us are going skating this evening. Can you come?"

Mollie glanced at the time, and made a face. "I wish I could, Sarah, but I've still got a ton of homework to catch up on, and my parents say that comes first."

"We'll miss you."

Mollie hung up the phone, feeling a nagging discontent. "So what?" she told Smokey, as the cat wound itself around her ankles, waiting to be petted. "I've got lots of excitement in my life right now—auditioning for a part in a television show, meeting big stars. What do I care if I'm missing hayrides and skating parties?"

She did care. Mollie stroked the gray and white fur and murmured to the cat, "You don't believe me, do you? I do care."

Monday morning Mollie struggled out of bed once more, thinking glumly that getting up early didn't get any easier with practice. She picked out her most becoming outfit, hoping to impress Ricky Thorne. In the car, she dozed all the way to the studio, but tried to look alert and ready to go when she scrawled her name on the sign-in sheet.

Would Ricky be on the set today? Would they be taping together again? Maybe he would make an excuse to come by early and see her. Surely today he would ask her to eat lunch with him.

Mollie was thankful to see her mother take her recipe folder and cookbook and sit down on a folding chair on the side of the set. Mollie, free to head for the dressing room on her own, dawdled in the hall, hoping that Ricky Thorne would be on the lookout for her.

It seemed that her wish had been granted. She turned the corner and saw Ricky waiting by the door to the makeup rooms, a large bouquet of flowers in his hand. He wore a simple white shirt with Mexican embroidery. It set off his dark hair and tanned skin, and Mollie thought he looked incredibly handsome. Just seeing him made her heart beat faster. She slowed her pace, thankful that she had spent extra time on her makeup that morning, despite the fact that it would be done over again at the studio. She smiled sweetly at the rock star.

"Oh, Ricky," she cooed, holding out her hand. "For me?"

Ricky stared at her, an unmistakable look of surprise on his face.

Just then the door to the makeup department opened, and a tall woman with long dark hair and large brown eyes walked out. She was elegantly dressed, even prettier than Nicole, and old—twenty-five at least, Mollie thought. The woman's face lit up at the sight of Ricky.

"Oh, Rick, you remembered!" She reached out

eagerly for the flowers, and buried her face in the fragrant blossoms.

Mollie jerked back her hand as if she'd touched a hot pan, and felt her face flood with crimson. How humiliating! He'd never meant the flowers for her at all. Mollie wished she could shut her eyes and go up in a wisp of smoke. She'd never been so embarrassed in her life.

"Happy birthday, Marna," Ricky said.

"And who is this—a young fan?" The woman smiled kindly at Mollie.

"This is—uh—Millie, isn't it?"

Mollie's face went from red to white, and she felt as if she'd stepped unwittingly into a cold shower. He didn't even remember her name! How fickle could a guy get?

"Mollie," she forced herself to say through stiff lips. "I—Rick and I worked together on Friday."

"Sure, I remember. You show a lot of promise, kid," the young rock star said. "Is it your birthday, too?"

Mollie looked blank for a moment, then realized that he was talking about the flowers, and she blushed all over again. "Quite a coincidence, isn't it?" she babbled. "I'd better go. See you later."

She hurried down the hall, risking one quick glance backward to see if they were laughing at her incredible blunder. But Marna was leaning close to Ricky, and the couple had obviously already forgotten her existence. Mollie groaned.

When she opened the door to the dressing room she shared with the other girls auditioning for the part, Mollie discovered the only other occupant was Roberta, as usual sitting in the corner with her head in a book, as if deliberately trying to ignore Mollie. Mollie had kept her distance from the unfriendly girl for several days, but today she had to talk to someone.

"Ricky Thorne was outside the makeup room with this gorgeous brunette," Mollie blurted.

Roberta didn't raise her head. "So? That's his girlfriend. She's got a part in another TV show. I'll bet she's shooting today."

"But—" Mollie felt betrayed. "When I was filming the test shoot on Friday with Ricky, he was so nice—he told me what to do and where to stand . . ."

"Yes," Roberta nodded. "He's a nice guy that way, easy to work with, and he always helps beginners."

"Oh-h," Mollie sighed, sinking down in one of the chairs. She wished she hadn't told all her friends at Vista High that Ricky was crazy about her. "He called me 'sweetheart,'" she reminded herself miserably.

"He calls everybody that." Roberta finally raised her head, looking curiously at Mollie. "You didn't think that it meant anything, did you?"

"Of course not," Mollie said loudly, looking at herself in the mirror, thinking how young she looked next to the perfectly made-up, gorgeous actress in the hall. Mollie felt like an utter fool. Trying to pull her thoughts away from her nonexistent love affair, she looked back at the other girl.

"Did you have a nice weekend?"

"Are you kidding?" Roberta answered irritably.

What did I say wrong now? Mollie thought. Bewildered, she blundered on. "Why not?"

"Look, I have acting lessons Saturday morning, two dance lessons Saturday afternoon, and voice on Sunday, okay?"

"Good grief." Mollie sounded startled. "When do you have time for fun?"

"I don't."

The other girl sounded so miserable that Mollie didn't know what to say. After a long pause, Mollie asked meekly, "Are we the only two girls left in the running for the part?"

"You got it."

Mollie took a deep breath—to be so close to success and yet so far! "Would you like to practice with me before they call us to the set?"

"No."

Mollie, rebuffed yet again, felt her friendly smile fade. "See you later."

She turned and stepped quickly outside the dressing room, pulling the door shut behind her.

What an icicle that girl was. Mollie started back toward the set, deciding she would sit with her mother and look over her lines while she waited for her call. She had taken only a few steps when she realized that she'd left her copy of the script in the dressing room.

Mollie frowned; she hated to face Roberta again, but she had to have her script. She'd just slip in quietly and then leave before Roberta could deliver another of her scorching putdowns.

Mollie walked quietly back to the dressing room and was about to pull open the door when a muffled sound made her pause. Someone was crying!

Chapter 13

$\mathcal{M}$ollie pushed open the door and barged in. Roberta had her face hidden in her hands, but looked up quickly when Mollie entered. Her expressing was forbidding, although it was obvious from her flushed face and swollen eyes that she was terribly unhappy. In her concern Mollie forgot to be intimidated.

"Roberta, what's wrong?"

"What do you care?" The other girl's tone was belligerent. "You'd be happy if I don't get the part."

Mollie flushed. "I know we'd both like to get the role, but I don't wish you any bad luck, honest. You're really good. I watched you work the other day."

"It may not matter if I'm good or not," Roberta sniffed, digging through her purse for a handkerchief.

"Why not?" Mollie asked, pushing a box of tissues toward the other girl, who pulled out a couple and dabbed at her tears.

"It's my grades. I failed a history exam before we began auditions. My teacher at school says she'll let me take it over, but if I can't bring my grade back up, I won't be able to get my work permit renewed, and then I won't be able to act."

Mollie, nonplussed, stared at the other girl. "I'm not the greatest in school either, Roberta, but really, history's not that hard. If you study . . ."

"I can't concentrate on history, worrying about this part." Roberta's face contorted as a new wave of tears threatened to overwhelm her. "I *need* this part, Mollie. I haven't done a commercial in three months, and my little brother hasn't had one in two."

"But surely . . ."

"My mother quit her job so she could be on the set with us when we were working." Roberta reached for another tissue, and sniffed hard. "I feel like I've let her down."

Mollie, beginning to see that more was involved here than she had suspected, shook her head. "Your dad . . ."

"They're divorced."

"Oh," Mollie said. "Your mother . . . did she like her job?"

"She was selling makeup. It wasn't that great," Roberta told her. "But now we need the money, Mollie. You don't have to worry about that, I bet."

Mollie felt a twinge of guilt at her good fortune, as she tried to get to the heart of the problem.

"Roberta, I don't really know your mother, but she seems like a nice lady. Does she know how upset you are?"

"Of course not," Roberta sniffed. "I didn't want her worrying, too."

"I bet she'd much rather go back to a boring job than have you worry yourself into a frazzle. If you relax, you can concentrate on your studying, and I bet you can bring up your grades."

"I've tried so hard, Mollie," Roberta sighed. "I feel like I'm permanently attached to this darned history book."

"That's why you never eat lunch with the rest of us," Mollie said, suddenly enlightened, "and why you always have your head in a book during breaks, never talking to anyone. I thought you were just stuck up."

Roberta managed a weak smile, and Mollie grinned back.

"Listen," she said, "what are you studying?"

"The Gold Rush."

"I studied that before Christmas," Mollie told her. "Why don't you let me help you? It's more fun than studying alone, and it might help you remember."

"Would you really do that?"

"Sure," Mollie told her, thinking, Better than sitting around mooning over Ricky and the romance that never was.

They spent the next hour in quiet harmony, while Mollie drilled Roberta on people, places, and dates. When the assistant director came to call them to the set, they put away the textbook and grabbed their scripts.

Mollie dreaded seeing Ricky Thorne again, so she hung back a little as they approached the set. Luckily, the rock star was nowhere to be seen, and a piano had been rolled to the side of the set. Mollie viewed the new addition with a sense of misgiving.

Ty Brenner, the young producer, and the bearded director were deep in conversation. They stopped talking when the two girls came onto the set.

"Hi, Mollie, Roberta." Ty smiled at them. "I have good news and bad news."

Mollie felt Roberta stiffen beside her, and she felt her own heart pounding. Was this the final cut? Who would they choose for the part? She took a deep breath.

"First," the producer told them, "I want to tell you that you've both done a splendid job, and I'm quite impressed with your abilities. Whomever we end up choosing for the role, I want you both to remember that we were very pleased with your work. Unfortunately, we can only use one girl in this pilot . . . and now there's a new wrinkle."

The girls stared at him, waiting for the ax to fall.

"The powers-that-be have decided that since Ricky is a singer, his 'younger sister' should be a singer, too. I'm sorry to throw this at you after all the tests we've done, but it wasn't my decision." He paused, preparing for the next part of his announcement. "I thought we'd just do a little impromptu singing today, nothing to get nervous about, and then take it from there."

Mollie looked from the man's friendly smile down to his expensive running shoes. She felt as if she'd walked into a brick wall. Singing!

Of course she'd sung in the fall musical at school, but Mollie would be the first to admit that she hadn't had an awful lot of competition. Besides, she knew it was her acting ability that had gotten her the part, not the quality of her voice, which was only average. She was doomed.

Then a thought struck her—maybe Roberta wasn't any better. Mollie brightened slightly.

"Who'd like to go first?"

Mollie and Roberta shared a panic-stricken glance, and Roberta gulped. "I will, if Mollie doesn't mind."

"Go ahead," Mollie told her generously, glad to postpone the inevitable. She stepped back and perched on one of the folding chairs, watching Roberta and the young producer at the piano.

"What would you like to sing?" the man asked, sitting down at the piano. "I'll try to bang out an accompaniment, if you don't mind a few goofs."

Roberta thought for a minute, then mentioned a popular ballad.

"I can do that," Mr. Brenner said. He touched the keys and the gentle melody began to flow.

Roberta took a deep breath and began to sing softly. Two stagehands paused to listen. The rest of the crew around the set became silent. Mollie, sitting stiff and tense in her chair, found that she was holding her breath.

Roberta was good. She had a pleasant, husky tone to her singing voice, and the clear, rich sound she produced made the last of Mollie's hopes fade.

Mollie could carry a tune and blend in well with a group, but she couldn't top this.

Mollie let her breath out in a long sigh, and saw all her big dreams go with it. No more makeup sessions, no wardrobes designed just for her, no more romantic scenes with a gorgeous hunk—although that part of the daydream had already been pretty well shot down. No more *Mollie Lewis, Hollywood star*!

Mollie pressed her lips together tightly. She'd be a good sport, she wouldn't let anyone know just how much it hurt to give up her dream. Roberta would do a good job with the part, and she'd worked hard for it.

Suddenly Mollie remembered Roberta's worries over her grades. If the other girl couldn't bring her grades back to a C average, she couldn't renew her work permit, and the producers couldn't use her no matter how badly they wanted her. If they knew that Roberta was so close to being unable to work, would they even consider her for the part?

As the vision of her name in gold letters on a dressing room door reappeared in Mollie's mind, she took a deep breath and looked up eagerly at the producer.

"Your turn, Mollie."

"Mr. Brenner," Mollie said, "there's something I think you should know."

Chapter 14

"**W**hat is it, Mollie?" The producer raised his brow.

Mollie hesitated, and looking past him she saw Roberta, her expression anxious. Roberta, who had worked so hard for this part, and who had trusted Mollie with her secret.

What are you doing, Mollie Lewis? some part of her mind demanded. Is this the kind of person you are? Is this part—is any part—worth turning into a snitch, or backstabbing someone who's become your friend?

Mollie knew the answer to her own question. She felt as if she'd come close to the edge of a deep pit, and barely glimpsed the precipice in time.

"Well, Mollie?"

"It's just—" Mollie floundered, "I mean, I'd like to have the role, Mr. Brenner. And I want you to know how much I've learned and how I appreciate the chance to try out. But I'm really not a singer."

Roberta breathed an audible sigh of relief as the producer said, "Thanks for being up front about it, Mollie, but why don't you try singing anyway? It would be a shame to have gone this far and not finish the audition."

"No, I don't think so," Mollie said. "But thanks for giving me the chance."

"Well, I'm sorry things turned out this way for you."

"Thanks," Mollie said, trying to keep her voice level. Behind him, she saw Roberta's face flush with happiness. Why shouldn't she be happy? Mollie asked herself. She wanted this as much as I did, if not more. It's not her fault I can't sing.

The other girl paused long enough to squeeze Mollie's hand.

"I'm sorry that we both couldn't get the part, Mollie."

Mollie nodded.

To her surprise, the producer turned back to her. "Mollie, I can't make any promises, but if our pilot gets picked up by the network, I'll keep you in mind for a guest shot, okay?"

Mollie's spirits instantly soared. "That would be great!" she cried. "Thanks, Mr. Brenner."

"Don't thank me," he said with a grin. "You're good, Mollie. Remember that."

He walked back to the rest of the crew, and the two girls headed across the set to where their mothers waited patiently. Roberta reached the women first with her good news.

Mollie watched Roberta hug her mother, and seeing the joy that lit up both faces, found that she couldn't feel too bad. Besides, they *might* call her back for a guest role.

Mrs. Lewis stood up as Mollie approached and gave her daughter a hug, too.

"I didn't get it," Mollie told her.

Laura Lewis nodded. "I gathered that. But I'm proud of you, Mollie. You handled all the extra work well, and you've behaved in a very mature and responsible manner. I think my baby is growing up."

Mollie frowned, not sure that she deserved this praise. "Thanks for all you and Dad did for me, even if I didn't get the part." She considered confessing just how close she had come to acting like a real skunk, but while she hesitated, her mother looked at her anxiously.

"Are you terribly disappointed, Mollie?"

"Not really," Mollie told her. "Mr. Brenner said he might be able to use me in a guest shot if the show is a success." She paused thoughtfully. "I've really missed being in on all the good times with my friends. I've even missed being at *school*," she finished. There was such a note of surprise in her voice that Mrs. Lewis laughed.

"Let's get your things and go home. It'll be nice to get back to a normal schedule."

"Yes," Mollie said. "If we hurry, I can get to school today before the last bell."

"My goodness." Mrs. Lewis raised her brows at

Mollie's zeal. "Did you really miss school *that* much?"

"No," Mollie admitted. "I want to tell Nicole and Cindy that I'm going to be a normal sister again. And, most of all, I've got to let David know that I'm available for the Valentine's Dance."

Here's a look at what's ahead in MAKING WAVES, the eighth book in Fawcett's "Sisters" series for GIRLS ONLY.

Cindy put her arms around Grant and kissed him. "That's for luck."

"I'll need lots of it."

"No problem. I got more where that came from." She kissed him again.

They walked into the school hand in hand. Cindy didn't even mind that she missed lunch. This conversation was much more important. She had decided that she would apologize to Ashley for jumping to conclusions. After all, Ashley was only helping Grant out as a good friend would.

Coming out of sixth period, Cindy glanced at her watch. If she hurried, she would catch Ashley before practice. "You on your way to the gym?" Duffy asked as he ran to catch up to her.

"Not yet. I've got to find Ashley first."

"How come?"

"I need to straighten something out," she said.

"I'll go with you," Duffy said, falling easily into step beside her.

"Thanks, but I need to do this alone. I'll meet you at the gym."

"Okay." He turned and went down the corridor to the gym. Cindy knew where Ashley would be. The new yearbook staff list was being posted after school outside the journalism room. She would bet that's where she was going to find both Ashley and Grant.

She saw Grant first. He was reading the list of names. Suddenly he jumped up and punched the air. "Yeah!" he shouted.

Cindy tried to push her way to him. He had gotten the editor's job. She was sure of it. But instead of breaking out of the crowd and rushing to her, he spun around and grabbed Ashley by the waist and lifted her high into the air. "We did it!" he yelled.

Ashley laughed and threw her arms around his neck. "Oh, Grant, I'm so proud of you. We'll have so much fun together on the yearbook. It's going to be great!" She put her hands on either side of his face and kissed him. Really kissed him. Cindy didn't know if Grant's look of surprise was because of the kiss or because he saw Cindy standing on the fringe of the crowd. She didn't wait to find out. Her cheeks flaming, she turned and ran blindly down the hall.

"Cindy, wait!" Grant yelled. But she had a good head start on him even though he was faster. Cindy ducked into the girls' locker room before he could stop her. He pounded on the door, yelling. "Cindy, if you don't get out here, I'm coming in!"

"Let him," she said, tears blinding her vision. She went out of the back door into the pool area and crashed into Duffy.

"Hey, what's wrong?"

"Everything," Cindy said. And for the first time in all the years they'd been friends, Cindy cried in Duffy's arms.